Praise for *Dic*

"*Dictionary Stories* brings t[...] mashup, digging in the c[...] them into new delights. This book remi[...] love and disappointment and deep humor, latent in our language and its storehouses; it just takes a keen eye to connect the dots. Jez Burrows is keen indeed."

—Robin Sloan, *New York Times* bestselling author of *Mr. Penumbra's 24-Hour Bookstore*

"The dictionary is not a place that you expect to find the stuff of romance, poignancy, belly laughs, or drama—unless you're Jez Burrows. He makes those flat samples of words in use shine and sparkle, knotting them together into vignettes that make you laugh, cry, gasp—vignettes that make language as personal as your own fingerprint. I write dictionaries, and I'll never look at their example sentences the same way again.

Dictionary Stories isn't just a book for word nerds, but for anyone for whom language and story matter. Everybody, A-Z, will find themselves thoroughly in love with this book."

—Kory Stamper, lexicographer and editor for Merriam-Webster, and author of *Word by Word*

"Jez has long been one of my favorite illustrators, and now he comes up with *Dictionary Stories*—sentences stolen from dictionaries and pasted together into tiny, delightful narratives. A brilliant literary remix."

—Austin Kleon, *New York Times* bestselling author of *Steal Like an Artist*

Dictionary
Stories

Dictionary Stories

Short Fictions and Other Findings

Jez Burrows

HARPER PERENNIAL

NEW YORK • LONDON • TORONTO • SYDNEY • NEW DELHI • AUCKLAND

HARPER ⬤ PERENNIAL

Cover illustrations: © Victorian Goods and Merchandise: 2,300 Illustrations (Carol Belanger Grafton), Dover Publications 1997 (peg, compass, die, flask, book, screw, gun, headless boy); 3200 Old-Time Cuts and Ornaments (Blanche Cirker), Dover Publications 2001 (eye, spiral stairs, tree, fish); © Animals: 1419 Copyright-Free Illustrations of Mammals, Birds, Fish, Insects, etc. (Jim Harper), Dover Publications 1979 (bird)

HarperCollins books may be purchased for educational, business, or sales promotional use. For information, please email the Special Markets Department at SPsales@harpercollins.com.

FIRST EDITION

Designed by Leydiana Rodriguez
Illustrated by Jez Burrows
Set in Tiempos Text and Tiempos Headline, by Klim Type Foundry

Library of Congress Cataloging-in-Publication Data has been applied for.

ISBN 978-0-06-265261-4 (pbk.)

18 19 20 21 22   LSC   10 9 8 7 6 5 4 3 2 1

Dedicated to my family,
and to the memory of
Kenneth Charles Isaac Burrows.

Contents

Bb

Cc

Dd

Ee

Ff

Gg

Hh

Ii

Jj

Kk

Ll

Mm

Nn

Oo

Pp

Qq

Rr

Ss

Tt

Uu

Vv

Ww

Xx

Yy

Zz

Introduction

Open this book to a random page and you could find yourself reading a noir thriller, a fantasy epic, a sci-fi romance, a family melodrama, a locker-room pep talk, a eulogy, a recipe, or a drawing-room murder mystery. Some stories take place over decades, while others are over in seconds. There are at least three talking animals, two sinister cults, and one headless ex-boyfriend. But while the subjects and forms of these stories are decidedly disparate, the stories themselves are unified by one constraint: each is composed entirely of example sentences taken from the dictionary. Twelve different dictionaries, to be precise.

If it's been a while since you last spent some quality time with one of the twelve dictionaries *you* own, here's a quick refresher on example sentences. Let's say, for reasons that are entirely your own business, you need to look up the definition of the word "murder." You open the *New Oxford American Dictionary*, skim over "mulberry" and "muntjac," pump the brakes and reverse when you hit "muscovado," until—*bull's-eye*. But before you can read the definition, your eye is caught by the strangely conspicuous italicized sentence that follows it—

Somebody tried to <u>murder</u> Joe.

If you're anything like me, you have questions: Who is Joe? Is Joe okay? What did Joe do to attract this sort of heat? Yet, sadly, Joe's story begins and ends in this humble example sentence. Katherine Connor Martin, head of US Dictionaries at Oxford University Press, writing on the *OxfordWords* blog, says the ideal example ". . . supports its definition by showing the word or sense in a typical grammatical and semantic context." So if the definition of the verb form of "murder" ("kill (someone) unlawfully and with premeditation") isn't sufficient, perhaps Joe's situation might cement the meaning for you.

There's a lot more that can be said about example sentences, but before we disappear down a lexicographic rabbit hole, I should probably first explain how I found myself using them to write the book you're currently reading. It started in the spring of 2015, when, while looking up the definition of "study" in the *New Oxford American Dictionary*, I found this:

> He perched on the edge of the bed, a <u>study</u> in confusion and misery.

Surrounded by the sober trappings of the dictionary, this sentence glowed with all the incongruity of a neon sign in a Renaissance painting. It had such a distinct narrative—it was as if a small piece of fiction had somehow wandered out of its own book and settled down in the dictionary (which, as it happens, is not a million miles from the truth, but more on that later). As I continued leafing idly through the pages of the *NOAD*, I found my eyes newly attuned to these restless sentences. They were sometimes hilarious, often melancholy or outright tragic, romantic, absurd, surprising, and occasionally quite inscrutable—and this edition boasted more than eighty thousand of them. I suddenly saw the dictionary in an entirely new light: a literary Trojan horse, outwardly presenting itself as a book of reference, while secretly transporting thousands of dismantled short stories. All of which led me to wonder—was it possible to put those stories back together? Settling into the cozy grip of procrastination, I went back to the entry for "study" and tried combining two of its examples:

He perched on the edge of the bed, a <u>study</u> in confusion and misery, a <u>study</u> of a man devoured by awareness of his own mediocrity.

I sat up in my seat. I had accidentally created a miserable little room and installed a sad sack tenant, and now I wanted to know more. I started looking for other sentences to complement those I had already found, and I discovered them under the entries for "bleak" and "untidy":

He perched on the edge of the bed, a <u>study</u> in confusion and misery, a <u>study</u> of a man devoured by awareness of his own mediocrity. He looked around the <u>bleak</u> little room in despair. The place was dreadfully <u>untidy</u>.

I took a moment to thank whichever cosmic deity had chosen to nudge me in the direction of this idea, took a deep breath, and got comfortable. I started furiously scanning the dictionary for examples, saving any that seemed as if they might spark a story. One modest text file with a handful of sentences soon grew into an unwieldy mess of files organized by category: sentences about time; sentences about family; sentences beginning with "I," "he," "she," or "they"; sentences shorter than six words; sentences in the form of a question . . .

I corralled and arranged sentences like a photographer herding wayward wedding guests into the frame, and soon found myself with a dozen short stories. I printed and bound a small run of Risograph zines for friends and anybody foolish enough to give me money for them on the internet, and simultaneously posted a few stories for free online.

Very soon after, hundreds of strangers—some of them kind journalists clearly fighting the boredom of a slow newsroom—started tweeting, sharing, and writing about them. I talked to bemused radio hosts at the CBC, and reporters at the *Washington Post* and It's Nice That. A reporter at *Slate* whom I didn't even have to bribe called them "existentially moving." I received messages from creative-writing tutors who were using the stories as an exercise with their students, and from stay-at-home parents playing them like a word game with their children at the breakfast table.

Six months passed, and to my surprise I woke to find that I had hoodwinked an agent into representing me and a publisher into publishing me. Faced with a contract to write a book of stories, I did what any rational person would do: quit my day job, and bought a dozen dictionaries.

I began with a list of themes. I decided that in deference to the source material, this book should be organized alphabetically by the sort of universal themes that great fiction concerns itself with: *D* for "dentistry," *H* for "horticulture," *N* for "nitroglycerin"—you know, the classics. However, I quickly discovered that writing to theme using found sentences is deceptively difficult. You might have the perfect story about dentistry in your back pocket, but you're out of luck unless you can find the sentences with which to construct it. I soon learned to submit to serendipity and let the dictionaries dictate what I would write on any given day. Today, professional golfers in the midst of a nervous breakdown; tomorrow, vengeful cross-dressing horn players.

Embracing chance proved to be fruitful. Not only did the dictionaries suggest themes, but as I mined the *New Oxford American Dictionary*, the *Macquarie Dictionary*, the *Collins English Dictionary*, and others for examples, I found that certain sentences also seemed to come prepackaged with a clear sense of genre, character, place, or time. There was no mistaking what I had to do with a sentence like "*The horses were lame and the men were tired*,"* or "*The double life of a freelance secret agent*."† When I found the textbook murder-mystery excerpt "*Where were you on the night when the murder took place?*"‡ it was simply a case of casting a very specific net for the vocabulary and narrative beats I knew I needed to complement it, while allowing for whatever serendipitous spanners the dictionary cared to throw into the machine.* I discovered that everything is mercurial in the face of a two-thousand-page book of everything on earth—stories would wax and wane, advance and retreat, turn on a thematic dime without warning. I thought of the unquestioning logic I used when I'd played with LEGO bricks as a kid: just as a doctor's office could become a twenty-four-hour drive-through giraffe sanctuary, so, too, could a story ostensibly about a romantic tryst in a hotel room become a story about artificial intelligence§—all because I dug around in the box and pulled out the right pieces.

Speaking of that giant box of literary LEGO bricks, now is probably the right moment to talk about where they originate, and whom we have to thank for them. The lexicographer

---

* "A Fistful of Feathers," 74.
† "Curtains," 28.
‡ "The Night in Question," 79.
§ "Some Vast Assemblage," 42.

is an often timorous and retiring breed, famously defined by Samuel Johnson (author of the 1755 *A Dictionary of the English Language*) as "a writer of dictionaries; a harmless drudge, that busies himself in tracing the original, and detailing the signification of words." One responsibility included in the detailing that Johnson mentions is the writing and sourcing of example sentences. Kory Stamper, a lexicographer for Merriam-Webster, in her book *Word by Word: The Secret Life of Dictionaries*, goes into detail about what constitutes an exemplary example:

> The point of example sentences in dictionaries isn't just to fill out space and drive lexicographers to a nervous breakdown but to help orient the user in terms of a word's broader context, its connotative meanings, its range, its tones. In all the things that people look for in writing—narrative, color, dialogue—it must be bland, yet it must be lexically illuminating, showing formality of tone and collocative use, sounding completely and utterly natural even if it is the most highly constructed sentence you've ever written. It's a difficult balance to get right.

Though terminology and approach differ from dictionary to dictionary, Stamper details the two broad categories that most examples fall into:

1. **Authorial quotations.** Often set apart from the definition and fully attributed, these are sentences plucked from existing works—typically books, journals, or newspapers.

2. **Verbal illustrations.** Sometimes referred to as "in-line example sentences," these unattributed examples can be written from scratch but are usually drawn from a corpus—an enormous database of written content sourced from blogs, news broadcasts, academic papers, and beyond. Search for a specific word, and the corpus will return a list of all its usages, from which lexicographers can pull a suitable example to use; or they can write one that represents the most common usage.

As I delved into the sentences' origin and construction, it became clear why certain example sentences seemed torn from the pages of other works—they actually *were*. Some cursory Google-assisted sleuthing revealed that one of my stories[*] contained sentences from: a 1972 *New York Times* article about Harvard's *National Lampoon*; John O'Hara's 1940 novel set in jazz-age Chicago, *Pal Joey*; and a *Playboy* interview with Tom Petty. I started having dreams about infinitely recursive books hidden inside books, like matryoshka dolls.

Shelves loaded with dictionaries and a database of categorized sentences growing by the day, I soon settled into an easy, cyclical rhythm of exploration, categorization, and construction. I would only later discover, thanks to the internet and some chance procrastination, that I had become an unwitting bibliomancer.

Is that my tumbleweed, or did you bring your own? I should explain.

---

[*] "Diane Smoked Jive," 32.

Place a book on its spine, let it fall open, close your eyes, and pick a passage at random. You have just practiced bibliomancy—a form of divination first recorded as early as the eighteenth century that treats sacred books like slot machines for spiritual guidance. Whether you consult the Bible, the Quran, or the I Ching, that random passage is thought to be the voice of your chosen deity gently ushering you toward enlightenment. We often assume that finding inspiration in books is a hidden, cerebral process of reading and contemplation; I fell in love with this idea that inspiration could also be forced out through such an overtly physical transaction, as neat as flipping a coin or shuffling a deck of cards. Bibliophiles (myself included) love to wax dustily about the tactile qualities of the printed page, so it seemed only right to take advantage of that physicality in order to find guidance. But since I had no burning existential queries to take care of, no reason to play Old Testament roulette, I wondered: Why limit divination to *sacred* books? Why not let an atlas tell you where to move? Or let the Yellow Pages find you a soul mate? Or let a dictionary, with its tens of thousands of narrative signposts, point you in the direction of a good story?

My blindly divined example sentences suggested not only narrative, theme, character, and genre, but also form. A fortuitous run of examples in the order *adjective noun* ("*blended whiskey*," "*desiccated coconut*," "*fancy molasses*") lead to an increasingly unhinged cocktail menu.* A collection of ailments ("*dullness of vision*," "*shortness of memory*," "*extremes of temperature*") coalesced into a list of side effects for the heart-

---

* "Seasonal Craft Cocktails," 103.

broken.* The only reason I found myself writing a halftime locker-room monologue† was that I found the example "*Listen up, everybody.*"

When story and form weren't forthcoming, I set myself creative constraints in order to coax them out: stories composed of twenty-six sentences, one from each lettered section of the dictionary, in order; stories using only sentences from the *A*, *B*, or *C* sections; stories using only sentences that begin with "I was . . ." or contain the word "sorry" or start with a number. Menus, lists, monologues, dialogues, track lists, prose, poetry—all of it thanks to flipping through the dictionary and knowing where to stop.

As I continued to court fortuity and herd sentences together, I began to notice a worrying trend. Every story—at the time largely full of short, disconnected, declarative sentences—was starting to sound like a robot attempting to emulate Hemingway. In the interests of experimentation, I started to throw in the odd preposition or conjunction in order to vary the tone and rhythm of the stories, but I felt a twinge of guilt: Was this allowed? What about contractions? Or punctuation? The smallest conjunction could completely change the relationship between two sentences—

> *My family needed the money, so I was <u>obliged</u> to work. I felt a <u>tug</u> at my sleeve.*

> *My family needed the money, so I was <u>obliged</u> to work,* **but** *I felt a <u>tug</u> at my sleeve.*

---

* "Breakup Side Effects," 66.
† "Pep Talk," 167.

I quickly realized that the neat thing about inventing your own writing constraint is that you get to define the rules that govern it.

THE RULES

1. A Dictionary Story is defined as any short piece of writing composed of example sentences taken from one or more dictionaries. For flow and readability, the following small edits to example sentences are allowed:
   - Punctuation (including, but not limited to, quotation marks, parentheses, apostrophes, commas, periods, hyphens, and dashes) may be added or removed.
   - Formatting (bolding, italicizing) may be added or removed.
   - Conjunctions, prepositions, or adverbs may be added *between* discrete sentences, but may not be inserted *into* sentences.
   - Contractions may be formed from existing words.
   - Pronouns and proper names may be altered.
   - Sentence tense may be altered.
2. The sum of all edits must constitute less than 5 percent of the final story.
3. All edits must leave individual sentences as functioning examples of the given word.

While Rule 1 may seem generous, with its liberal allowance for edits, Rules 2 and 3 were designed to keep me honest, and the stories faithful to the constraint. Under these guidelines, I could change the sentence *"His voice was <u>rough</u> with barely suppressed fury"* to *"**Her** voice **is** <u>rough</u> with barely suppressed fury,"* as the changes in gender and tense do little to alter the sentence as an example of the word "rough." But I couldn't go as far as "His husky voice, rough with barely suppressed fury" or "Rough with fury barely suppressed, his voice" or "Seriously, you wouldn't believe how rough Steve's voice was." Every story in this book observes these rules, and should you wish to experiment with writing dictionary stories of your own, feel free to arm yourself with them.

Spend the better part of a year reading and reconfiguring the dictionary to write a book of stories, and you'll emerge on the other side with more than just paper cuts and a modestly enhanced vocabulary. You'll remember how inspiration and small pleasures can hide in plain sight, patiently waiting for a keen coconspirator to spring them loose. You'll find intimate connections between seemingly impossible bedfellows, and the universe will suddenly seem more knowable, if only for a second. You'll discover the words "famulus," "flocculent," and "minibeast," then sadly realize that, in all likelihood, you'll never be able to drop them into casual conversation. You'll possibly have a panic attack at three in the morning one Tuesday, and when asked by the doctor what you do for a living and if you've been under any abnormal stress lately, you'll quickly change the subject. For the most part, however, you'll stand on the shoulders of unwitting lexicographers to play six degrees of separation with the literary cosmos, and reaffirm for yourself the wild, elastic potential of language. Then you'll look up from your desk well after midnight to realize how profoundly lucky you are to have spent months of your life gleefully mucking around with other people's words, and getting the opportunity to share all of it with more people than you could hope to meet in a lifetime.

And then you'll never look at another dictionary for as long as you live.

(I'm kidding. Mostly.)

A Note on the Dictionaries

The interesting thing you discover when you start acquiring multiple dictionaries—beyond an exciting new awareness of lower-back pain—is how idiosyncratic they can be for books with a common goal. Each has a sense of personality, implicitly communicated through their covers, their interior layout and typography, their paper stock, their illustrations, and, naturally, their words, definitions, and examples.

I wrote the first two dozen stories for this project exclusively with the *New Oxford American Dictionary*, before I wondered: Would using other dictionaries significantly alter the stories I was writing? Could you identify a story written with one dictionary over another? Every story in this book is annotated with the dictionaries used to write it, so maybe you'll be able to answer those questions for yourself. Listed below are all the dictionaries referenced in this book, in the order they were acquired.

1. ***New Oxford American Dictionary***
   Third edition, 2010, Oxford University Press
   NOAD, which is what you're allowed to call the *New Oxford American Dictionary* when you know it as intimately as I do, enjoys a level of ubiquity possibly unmatched by the other dictionaries in this list, being the default dictionary referenced by most Macs and iPhones. It has it all: full sentences ("*The team*

has been _researching into flora and fauna_"), short fragments and clauses ("_a torrential downpour_"), dialogue ("_'It's OK, we're not related,' she joked_"), insults ("_You miserable old creep_"), terminology from philosophy, botany, geology, zoology, music, and sports, and much more.

2. Collins COBUILD Primary Learner's Dictionary

Second edition, 2014, HarperCollins Publishers

An attempt to find something in stark contrast to _NOAD_ led me next to Collins's _Primary Learner's Dictionary_, a British volume intended for primary-school students age seven and above. Given the intended audience, the word list is simpler and more concise than those of other dictionaries, and its examples are generally short and simply constructed, although the content is often no less adult. I'm sure "_She came into the room, almost completely nude_" is indispensable in the classroom.

3. Macquarie Dictionary

Revised third edition, 2001, The Macquarie Library Pty Ltd

The _Macquarie Dictionary_ is generally considered to be the authoritative source on Australian English. Macquarie refers to its examples as "illustrative phrases," and includes a wealth of region-specific vocabulary and thousands of diverse quotations from Australian writers. It also boasts a tremendous number of short fragments ("_lost ships_," "_for the time being_," "_a sudden attack_"), which proved useful when I was playing with the rhythm of stories.

4. ***Dictionary of American Slang, Barbara Ann Kipfer, PhD, and Robert L. Chapman, PhD***
Fourth edition, 2008, HarperCollins Publishers
I can't believe I wasted so many hours as a young boy looking through regular dictionaries for dirty words when I could have picked up a slang dictionary and found enough filth to sink a battleship. In addition to obscenities, *American Slang* is loaded with forties and fifties colloquialisms that would be more at home in a pulpy gumshoe thriller, such as "*You're the <u>dirty dog</u> that snuffed my brother.*"

5. ***NTC's Dictionary of British Slang and Colloquial Expressions, Ewart James***
1996, NTC Publishing Group
Problematic reading abounds in this volume, which boasts more filth and an embarrassment of best-ignored sexist, racist, and homophobic slurs. Avoid those, however, and you might be rewarded with something like the suspiciously P. G. Wodehouse–esque "*You may call it a <u>tumble in the hay</u>, my dear. I call it adultery!*"

6. ***The American Heritage Dictionary of Idioms, Christine Ammer***
1997, Houghton Mifflin Company
I found this dictionary in San Francisco's own Mechanics' Institute Library, and fell in love as soon as I found the sentence "*Can he <u>make a living</u> as a*

freelance trumpeter?" Stories composed entirely of idioms are hard to write and miserable to read, so I generally dipped into this dictionary when stories required a little colloquial secret sauce.

7. *Collins English Dictionary*

Seventh edition, 2015, HarperCollins Publishers
With contemporary British English for young readers covered by Collins's *Primary Learner's Dictionary*, I knew I needed a modern adult volume to pair it with. *Collins English Dictionary* is a stout and densely packed edition with mercifully legible typesetting, and its examples seem to prize brevity above all else. Occasionally, though, it whips out a line like *"The light percolating through the stained-glass windows cast colored patterns on the floor.'"*

8. *The Home Book of Proverbs, Maxims and Familiar Phrases, Burton Stevenson*

First edition, 1948, The Macmillan Company
The oldest dictionary referenced in this collection is a literary bird's nest of quotations organized by theme, from "ability" to "zeal," with choice words from Shakespeare, Byron, Voltaire, Thomas Jefferson, Adam Smith, and more, compiled by American anthologist Burton Egbert Stevenson. (Go ahead and say his name out loud a few times. I'll wait.) My copy is a handsome clothbound beast in a hard slipcase, with a smell that would set print fetishists quivering.

---

* "Mother Lode," TK.

9. ***The American Heritage Dictionary of the English Language***
Fifth edition, 2016, Houghton Mifflin Harcourt Publishing Company
A formidable—and wonderfully designed—dictionary, and the most recent referenced in this book, the *American Heritage Dictionary* shares *New Oxford American*'s sheer breadth of example constructions and specialized terminology—from astronomy to cartography, dancc to Egyptology.

10. ***Merriam-Webster's Collegiate Dictionary***
Eleventh edition, 2003, Merriam-Webster Inc.
An embarrassingly late addition to the roster, given that Merriam-Webster is the oldest dictionary publisher in the US and the *Collegiate* is perhaps the most popular desk dictionary in the country. Merriam-Webster's approach to examples is remarkably buttoned-down, compared to that of many of the dictionaries in this list—they're short and efficient, and have a distinct no-nonsense tone.

11. ***My First Dictionary, Archie Bennett***
Third edition, 1989, Delair Publishing Company
Equal parts charming and creepy, *My First Dictionary* is an illustrated dictionary for the very young based on a list of 1,500 words taken from the *New Webster's Dictionary of the English Language*. Its examples are slight, simple, and full of Bills, Toms, Janes, and Marys.

12. *Black's Law Dictionary*, Bryan A. Garner

Fifth pocket edition, 2016, West Publishing Co.
An abridged version of the most widely used law
dictionary in the United States. Examples are thin
on the ground and written with a uniform court-
room formality, veering between dense jargon
("*there is no need for intendment, the court reasoned,
when the text of the statute is clear*") and strangely
poignant fragments ("*alienation of affections*," "*so-
lemnity of marriage*").

Please note: Every dictionary referenced in this book was
compiled using its own unique style guide. Those guides dictate every formatting decision from hyphenation to capital-
ization, abbreviation, the treatment of names and numbers,
and far beyond. To combine excerpts from all twelve of those
dictionaries with no thought to unifying those formatting
choices would leave these stories much worse for wear. Con-
sequently, in addition to those edits mentioned in The Rules,
further small edits have been made throughout this book in
the interests of maintaining the publisher's house style, and
ensuring the best reading experience. Perhaps most nota-
bly—at least to this Englishman—UK spellings have been altered to their US counterparts. This pains me as much as it
does you, British readers. Feel free to pencil all the missing *u*'s
back in to "color" and "favor" as you see fit.

Dictionary
Stories

Aa

Aggression, Passive

John

The English <u>language</u> has over five hundred thousand words, but John didn't say a <u>word</u> all the way home.

Source: *New Oxford American Dictionary*

You Have Five New Messages

Hey, <u>you</u>! I've been trying to <u>reach</u> you all morning! <u>What's happening</u>? How's it going? How did the weekend <u>go</u>? You <u>must</u> be tired. I <u>hope</u> that the kids are OK. I spent the <u>majority</u> of the day reading, then I went for a <u>long</u> walk—the path <u>along</u> the cliff? Oh, but I'm such a silly <u>goose</u>, I lost my—you know—my <u>doodad</u>—my watch. All right, I'll give you a <u>ring</u> later. I love you, darling.

Hey, <u>you</u>! <u>How goes it</u>? Everything okay? I just called to say <u>hey</u>. It's cold and <u>wet</u> outside, and your father misses you <u>terribly</u>. Did you sleep <u>well</u> last night? I woke up in the <u>middle</u> of the night and heard a noise outside. I won't <u>keep</u> you; I know you've got a busy evening. Call me <u>when</u> you're finished? I love you, darling.

Hey, you. Where in the world have you been? Are you all right, love? Telephone me as soon as you can. It's always great to hear from you. I love you.

Hey. You. It's ten past eleven. I haven't heard from my daughter in two weeks. If you can give me a few minutes of your time I'll be much obliged.

Hey, you. I'm very sorry, I really am. I know my temper gets the better of me at times. This time of year always depresses me. I realize now that I've been very selfish. I love you, darling. I will always love you, whatever happens.

Sources: *New Oxford American Dictionary, Collins COBUILD Primary Learner's Dictionary, The American Heritage Dictionary of Idioms, NTC's Dictionary of British Slang*

Animals

Fawns

She drove at a <u>furious</u> speed, the baby deer <u>nestled</u> in her arms. The night skies were <u>somber</u> and starless, and it was <u>beginning</u> to snow. The cut was <u>bleeding</u> steadily.

She wore a <u>sloppy</u> sweater and jeans, a laboratory <u>coat</u>, and an <u>ID</u> card. Her <u>eyes</u> were swollen with crying. She <u>joined</u> the department last year, the <u>apex</u> of her career. But something out of the ordinary was <u>afoot</u>—a <u>no-man's-land</u> between art and science. Her mind <u>sheer</u>ed away from images she didn't want to dwell on: <u>field</u> observations; a yellow-<u>beaked</u> alpine chough; a <u>stagnant</u> ditch; a hairline <u>crack</u> down the middle of a glass; a <u>pool</u> of blood.

Sleep still eluded her.

Her self-control finally broke. Sat up all night, laced a guard's coffee with a sedative, and made a break for the door.

A beam of light flashed in front of her, and smoke appeared on the horizon. She suddenly went cold with a dreadful certainty. A sob escaped her lips. She tried to compose herself. She wouldn't put it past him to lay a trap for her.

Sources: *New Oxford American Dictionary, Merriam-Webster's Collegiate Dictionary*

Apocalypse, The

The Barrens

Crossing the barrens was no easy feat. Border patrols, burial mounds, mines, booby traps, and underground fortifications. The map didn't seem to bear any relation to the roads. I took a supply of coffee and cigarettes to use as barter, and bivouacked on the north side of town, the rain belting down on the tin roof. My jeans had patches on the knees, like badges of courage marking encounters with barbed wire.

The day before was a blur. I remember a buzzing in my ears, a burning building, bullets bounding off the veranda. Further attacks by the mob. The bombers began to come nightly, and the city was blacked out. Guerrillas continued to besiege the other major cities to the north. There seems no end to the bestiality of human beings. We need rainfall of biblical proportions to bring us back to normal.

The road branched off at the town. There was the terminal and, beyond, an endless line of warehouses. The runways had cracked open, exposing the black earth beneath. All the doors were locked and bolted, but the explosion blasted out hundreds of windows.

The climb left me breathless. Inside, I barricaded the door with a bureau and braced myself for the inevitable blast. Drums were beating in the distance. I knew when I was beaten.

Source: *New Oxford American Dictionary*

Seven Sisters

It was still night when we <u>hit</u> the outskirts of Chicago. The woods were still and <u>silent</u>. The power lines had been brought down by <u>falling</u> trees. Derelict houses were <u>abandone</u>d. We <u>camp</u>ed out for the night in a mission schoolroom.

Sophie got Beth to <u>make</u> a fire. Lucy <u>saw</u> to it that everyone got enough to eat. Bella <u>sang</u> to the baby. Virginia had a sick feeling in her <u>stomach</u>. Ruth did her <u>best</u> to reassure her.

We all scared real <u>easy</u> in those days. We <u>were</u> everything to each other.

I'll have that coffee now, if the offer still <u>holds</u>.

Source: *New Oxford American Dictionary*

Art

Portrait of the Artist As a Stubborn Old Fool

I've had an <u>argument</u> with my father. (An <u>old</u> tradition.) At my <u>suggestion</u>, the museum held an exhibition of his work: a collection of <u>sculpture</u>, a series of charcoal <u>drawings</u> on white paper, canvases characterized by lively, flowing <u>brushwork</u>. He's a <u>one-off</u>, no one else has his skills. His mystical philosophy <u>permeates</u> everything he creates. He's greatly respected by his

peers in the arts world, but I don't believe he gave the industry a fair shake.

He was livid at being left out of the planning—"I can manage alone, thanks all the same." There was a heated exchange, each side waiting for the other to blink, as per usual.

My father nurtured my love of art: abstract painting and sculpture, photography, traditional Japanese wood-block printmaking . . . He taught me everything I know. But he can be a cantankerous old fossil at times—a stout man with a florid face, polishing the furniture and making everything just so. Ultimately, he has only himself to blame. He is drinking far too much these days. Even Lawrence finally lost patience with him. At his age, I guess he doesn't frighten anymore.

Sources: *New Oxford American Dictionary, Collins English Dictionary, The American Heritage Dictionary, Merriam-Webster's Collegiate Dictionary*

Assassination

Hunter

He perched on the edge of the bed, a <u>study</u> in confusion and misery, a <u>study</u> of a man devoured by awareness of his own mediocrity. He looked around the <u>bleak</u> little room in despair. The place was dreadfully <u>untidy</u>—tattered notebooks filled with illegible <u>hieroglyphics</u>, the <u>mysteries</u> of analytical psychology, Victorian <u>architecture</u>, graphic pictures of torture and <u>dismemberment</u> . . . The streetlamps shed a faint <u>light</u> into the room. It was beginning to <u>rain</u>.

The woman in the <u>next</u> room listened to the <u>rhythm</u> of his breathing. She sat very <u>still</u>, her eyes closed. She heard the <u>click</u> of the door and a <u>clockwork</u> motor, before he was thrown backward by the <u>force</u> of the explosion.

All their married life, she had been living a <u>lie</u>. She brushed back a curl that had strayed from its <u>bonds</u>.

Her hunting days were <u>done</u>.

Source: *New Oxford American Dictionary*

Babysitting

Ten Dollars an Hour and Whatever You Want from the Fridge

"Hello <u>there</u>! Come <u>in</u>. Thanks very much for your <u>help</u>.

"The children go to bed <u>at</u> nine o'clock—no ifs, buts, or <u>maybe</u>s. Make sure the baby isn't sleeping in an <u>awkward</u> position. Make sure the children's hands are <u>clean</u> before they eat, and don't put the potato skins down the <u>garbage disposal</u>. These foods are <u>strictly</u> forbidden: chocolate <u>eggs</u>, <u>chocolate</u> pudding, chocolate cake filled with whipped cream and topped with hot <u>fudge</u>, hair <u>gel</u>. Julia and Lydia are <u>identical twins</u>. Upstairs is off-limits, <u>capeesh</u>? Don't <u>go</u> poking your nose where you shouldn't. Please don't let the fire go <u>out</u>, don't <u>overexpose</u> the children to television, and do not <u>admonish</u> little Stanislaus if he tears the heart out of a backyard sparrow; he took the divorce <u>hard</u>. We recycle <u>aluminium</u> cans.

"If you have any <u>queries</u>, please do not hesitate to contact me. I'll be home before <u>dark</u>. <u>Here</u>'s the money I promised you, a <u>fifth</u> of whiskey, a list of <u>forbidden</u> books, and a <u>bulletproof</u> vest. Thanks, I <u>owe</u> you one for this."

Sources: *New Oxford American Dictionary, Collins COBUILD Primary Learner's Dictionary, Macquarie Dictionary, The American Heritage Dictionary*

Blasphemy

Genesis 1

In the beginning, <u>God</u> created heaven and the earth. Then came a lot of <u>titillating</u> tabloid speculation and <u>slanderous</u> allegations: he was <u>stepping</u> out with a redheaded waitress, and he was in debt to the <u>tune</u> of $40,000. He pled not <u>guilty</u> to murder, and insisted that the cocaine in the glove compartment was a <u>plant</u>. He was found guilty of <u>mismanagement</u> of public funds and sentenced to six hundred hours of community service. He went into <u>self-imposed</u> exile, and after a while, the noise <u>died</u> down. The scandal had no <u>discernible</u> effect on his career.

Sources: *New Oxford American Dictionary*, *Macquarie Dictionary*

The Lord's Prayer, From Memory

<u>Heavenly</u> Father,
What a <u>great</u> guy.
<u>Keep</u> up the good work,
Magic, supernatural powers, and the <u>like</u>.
I <u>beg</u> forgiveness,
I <u>swear</u> by all I hold dear that I had nothing to do with it.
<u>Deliver</u> us from evil,
Or <u>point</u> me in the right direction,

Let's all get the <u>hell</u> out of here.

<u>Amen</u> to that.

Sources: *New Oxford American Dictionary, Collins English Dictionary, Macquarie Dictionary*

Budgeting

Dinah

Dinah looked <u>enchanting</u>. She was <u>full</u> of confidence. She felt <u>exultant</u> and powerful. Decked out in furs, she was <u>mounted</u> on a white horse, and her dress <u>billowed</u> out around her, blue silk <u>embellished</u> with golden embroidery and <u>yards</u> and yards of fine lace. She wore a <u>string</u> of agates around her throat, a necklace of <u>cabochon</u> rubies, a bracelet <u>set</u> with emeralds. Everybody was listening <u>intently</u>. They <u>gaped</u> at her as if she were an alien.

"I have a confession to make," she announced. The last notes of the symphony died away. "We have used all the available funds."

She coughed discreetly.

Sources: *New Oxford American Dictionary*, *Merriam-Webster's Collegiate Dictionary*

Business

The Cursing of Gregory Hardware

He was a <u>stand-up</u> kind of guy, a nice old gentleman, but <u>not buttoned-up too tightly</u>, as you noticed. He was so vain, it was easy to <u>set him up</u>. Listen to <u>this</u>: he believed that an evil spirit put a <u>curse</u> on his business. It was all lies! I <u>made</u> it all up. And he fell for it! What a <u>sap</u>! He took my <u>advice</u> and put his house up for sale, sold the car in <u>part exchange</u> for another vehicle, and <u>parcel</u>ed up his only winter suit to take to the pawnbroker. He took his <u>stuff</u> and went. <u>Personally</u>, I think he made a very sensible move.

    <u>Hey</u>, I'm only human. I'm <u>sorry</u> he's gone. Anyway, who <u>gives a fuck</u>, actually? Business is <u>booming</u>. <u>Cutting throats</u> is the best way of cutting costs.

Sources: *New Oxford American Dictionary*, *Collins COBUILD Primary Learner's Dictionary*, *Dictionary of American Slang*

Cc

Celebrity

Harry Potter and the Once-in-a-Lifetime Business Opportunity in Southern California

I was doing the <u>iron</u>ing when he called—the actor Daniel Radcliffe, who plays the <u>hero</u> in the Harry Potter films. He asked <u>me</u> to go to California with him. He plans to <u>plant</u> fruit trees. It was a very <u>difficult</u> decision to make, but my job was making me <u>miserable</u>, and <u>citrus</u> fruits are a good source of vitamin C.

Source: *Collins COBUILD Primary Learner's Dictionary*

Cookery

Recipe

Here's a dish that is simple and quick to make:

Slice the onion into rings. Heat the oil until it just smokes. When the oil is hot, add a clove of garlic, and fry the onions until they are brown. Blend the onions, sugar, and oil to a paste, and grind some pepper into the sauce. Boil the potatoes until well-done. Cook the carrots in boiling salted water.

Break the chocolate into pieces. Put the meat under a grill until it is brown. Trim any excess fat off the meat and chop off the fishes' heads and tails—give the hair a quick pull, and it comes out by the roots. Grill the trout for about five minutes. Flake the fish. Dice the peppers. Sift the flour into a bowl and rub in the fat. Stand back and try to take a more objective view of your life as a whole. Let your Taurean stubbornness guide you. Add a smidgen of cayenne.

Divide the pastry in half and roll out on a surface dusted with flour. Take the marzipan and mold it into a cone. Broil until the nuts have toasted. Whip the cream until it is thick, and before the eggs begin to set, use the icing to model a house. Bake until golden. Give thanks to the Lord. Carefully peel away the wax paper, and scatter the coconut over the icing. Do not make the concrete too sloppy. Add the juice of a lemon, a few grains of corn, a ripe brie, and gallons of fake blood. Take an aspirin and lie down. Prepare the site, then lay an <u>even</u> bed of mortar, <u>set</u> the table, put the sausage on top of the polenta; then <u>dig</u> in.

Sources: *New Oxford American Dictionary*, *Collins COBUILD Primary Learner's Dictionary*, *Collins English Dictionary*

Correspondence

Why I Cannot Attend Your Baby Shower

I'm a busy woman.
I'm very pressed for time.
I have to be up insanely early.
I have a job that involves a lot of travel.
I have a shitload of work to do this week.
I have booked a table at the Swan.
I'm supposed to be meeting someone at the airport.
I'm expecting company.
I'm afraid of dogs.
I have an ingrowing toenail.
I'm convinced there is something fishy going on.
I think there's something to this alien business.
I have nothing against you personally.
I just want to get baked and watch a movie.
I'm very lazy by nature.
I'm majorly depressed.
I can't think of a better answer offhand.

Source: *New Oxford American Dictionary*

Why You Are No Longer Invited to Our Baby Shower

You and I are <u>through</u>.

You have a nerve, I must <u>say</u>.

You and I <u>see</u> things differently.

You are a <u>rustic</u> half-wit.

You're an arrogant little <u>toad</u>.

You have <u>disgrace</u>d the family name.

You're making a <u>terminal</u> ass of yourself.

You have a very <u>inflated</u> opinion of your worth.

You are the most buttoned-up <u>tight-arse</u> that I have ever met.

You have <u>singularly</u> failed to live up to your promises.

You're so damned self-righteous, you make me <u>sick</u>.

You look like a drowned rat—nothing <u>personal</u>.

You <u>rip</u>ped my jacket.

Source: *New Oxford American Dictionary*

Cults

The Last Toast

The hall was <u>rattling</u> with excitement. Hughie looked all around with a burning smile, <u>promising</u> all the entertainment of their lives. A stout <u>fella</u>, popular <u>among</u> the people. His life on the surface appeared joyous, full of novelty, <u>mad-cap</u> gaiety, intellectual challenge. But he did not like, although he thought himself a radical, to feel himself outside the comfort of the <u>fold</u>, to feel <u>lonesome</u>.

He padlocked the door for good <u>measure</u>. Bad <u>form</u> to <u>forsake</u> one's friends, to leave a room without <u>ceremony</u>. <u>Un</u>-heard-of. We've come this <u>far</u>—why turn back? We must all be prepared to make <u>sacrifices</u>. A <u>rush</u> of blood to his face, he cleared a <u>way</u> through the throng of people. Now the day of reckoning had come—sharp and sudden, with a <u>vengeance</u>. Be <u>upstanding</u> and charge your glasses.

Sources: *New Oxford American Dictionary, Macquarie Dictionary*

Dating

Date Night of the Living Dead

They sat looking at each other <u>without</u> speaking.

"What's the <u>matter</u>?"

"Me? <u>Oh</u>, I'm fine." She took a <u>sip</u> of the red wine and looked around <u>desperately</u>.

Like <u>hell</u>, he thought. He paused for a moment, as if <u>mar-shaling</u> his thoughts.

"Well, I just checked my watch and it's definitely <u>wine o'clock</u>."

He laughed at his own <u>pleasantry</u>. She <u>stifle</u>d a desire to turn and flee. There was a <u>strained</u> silence; all she could hear was the <u>pounding</u> of her heart, the <u>clinking</u> of glasses. Feeling the blush <u>mount</u> in her cheeks, she looked down quickly.

"I never seem to say the right thing, <u>do</u> I?" He put the question with <u>deceptive</u> casualness. She <u>swallow</u>ed a mouthful slowly.

"This wine is really <u>drink</u>ing beautifully."

"Oh, for God's <u>sake</u>!" snarled Dyson. "I <u>sometimes</u> wonder whether you really and truly love me, I <u>shit</u> you not. What am I doing <u>wrong</u>?"

She <u>paused</u>, at a loss for words. The door opened <u>softly</u>, and the <u>living dead</u> slowly ambled forward, with one leg dragging behind. Ginny <u>glance</u>d at her watch.

Source: *New Oxford American Dictionary*

Exes, An Incomplete List

1. A <u>minor</u> poet (He <u>wrote</u> under a pseudonym. We met through the <u>lonely hearts</u> ads.)
2. A <u>mediocre</u> actor (Camera-<u>shy</u>. Shockingly bad <u>manners</u>.)

3. The man who <u>lodged</u> in the room next door (A
   conveniently <u>situated</u> hotel. I didn't have the <u>heart</u>
   to tell him.)
4. A former Washington DJ whose <u>handle</u> was "Fat
   Daddy" (A man who, by his own <u>admission</u>, fell in
   love easily. We soon <u>ran out</u> of gas.)
5. A <u>retired</u> teacher (Pain<u>ful</u>.)
6. A topiary <u>gardener</u> (Dulls<u>ville</u>.)
7. The <u>Honorable</u> Richard Morris, Esquire, chief justice
   of the supreme court of our state (<u>No</u> comment.)
8. A <u>brilliant</u> young mathematician (A state <u>secret</u>.
   He kept <u>shtum</u> about the fact that he was sent
   down for fraud; then he <u>faked</u> his own death.)
9. A <u>manlike</u> creature (The effects of too much <u>drink</u>.
   I was feeling <u>low</u>.)
10. A lady chef (I just <u>knew</u> it was something I wanted
    to do. I was living in Cairo <u>then</u>.)
11. A double agent who <u>betrayed</u> some four hundred
    British and French agents to the Germans
    (<u>Unbelievable</u> or not, it happened. <u>Listening devices</u>
    were found in his private office. The man was wanted
    in a dozen countries but was as slippery as an <u>eel</u>.)
12. An army officer of fairly high <u>rank</u> (We were both
    <u>awfully</u> busy; he liked his <u>steak</u> rare. <u>Honestly</u>,
    that's all I can recall.)
13. A highly <u>esteemed</u> scholar (We were lucky enough
    to walk by the lions' enclosure at <u>feeding time</u>, when
    he said he "didn't care about life, so why should he
    <u>fear</u> death?" A <u>profoundly</u> disturbing experience.)

Sources: *New Oxford American Dictionary, Collins English Dictionary*

Death

Eulogy

My father was a great one for buying gadgets. A tall man with widely spaced eyes. A cheerful pipe-smoking man of ruddy complexion.

He was born in Seattle. At the age of sixteen he left home, a kid with no more idea of what to do than the man in the moon. He worked as an apprentice blacksmith, station hand, and finally station manager. He spent a year in the wilds of Canada. He dined outdoors, comforted by the crackling sounds of the fire. He loved the quietness and stillness of early summer days.

He had a phobia about being underwater. A phobia of germs. A snake phobia.

He married a lass from Yorkshire, and he fathered three children. One of my earliest memories is of sitting on his knee, bouncing up and down on the mattress.

Okay, that's it, you've cried long enough. Come on, silly.

He never talked at you. He never hogged the limelight. He was lavish with his hospitality. He was very giving and supportive. He spoke fluent Spanish, and he wrote almost every day. He was a model husband and father, and a tenacious local legend.

His bicycle was found close to the start of a forest trail.

I thought the world of my father. You don't get men like

him <u>anymore</u>. We're in <u>sore</u> need of him. I would write to him if I <u>knew</u> his address.

Source: *New Oxford American Dictionary*

Worst Picnic Ever

For <u>want</u> of a better location, we ate our picnic lunch in the cemetery. She <u>buttered</u> the toast; the coffin was lowered into the <u>grave</u>.

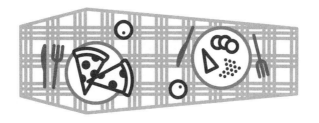

Source: *New Oxford American Dictionary*

Deception

Curtains

The double life of a freelance secret agent? My nerves are shot. This is all getting too deep for me. At about ten at night, I got a call. A cold, dead voice. He told me my telephones were tapped and I was being watched—they see me as a traitor, a sellout to the enemy.

I never thought Stash would rat on me. Times have changed. He had seen which way the wind was blowing. How cold and calculating he was. Little did he know what wheels he was putting into motion.

Trusting to the cover of night, I ventured out. I went to see Caroline, but nobody was at home. The garden was overgrown and deserted. Mary had vanished without a trace. Lizzie seemed to have vanished into thin air, as if her presence were merely notional. I should never have trusted her.

My own friends sold me down the river. A cabal of dissidents. A pack of wolves baying at the moon. It looked like curtains for me.

Source: *New Oxford American Dictionary*

Dutch's Last Agony

It was a wild night, pitch-black, with howling gales. The owl, for all his feathers, was acold. In achromatic gloom, garments drenched with rain, the men got hold of the coffin and levered at it with crowbars, threatening to tear it off its hinges.

Dutch's face darkened with gathering fury, piercing eyes glittering beneath a great beetling brow. Drunk with whiskey, he pictured Benjamin waiting—the still body of the young man, his hairless chest and his bloodless lips. In the hinterland of his mind these things rose, dark and ominous: Masked dancers. Shamanic rituals. Powdered rhino horn. He saw a kind-looking Aborigine holding out to him the biggest sugar bag he had ever seen. These visions appeared, unsummoned, the offspring of delirium. He dug his heel into the ground and wept aloud. The men scowled and muttered obscenities.

Suddenly, he saw the light. Some devilry was afoot. Unable to believe that what he saw was real, he took a step backward, when he received a blow to the skull and fell with a thud that left him winded. The lid was put into position and bolted down, and the coffin was lowered into the grave.

The men scaled a wall, a bottle of rum was opened, and they took a good long snort. Eight down and two to go.

Sources: *New Oxford American Dictionary, Collins English Dictionary, Macquarie Dictionary, Merriam-Webster's Collegiate Dictionary*

Depression

Customers Who Bought This Item Also Bought

Public Speaking for the Unemployed

Biblical Quotations for the Unemployed

Meditative Techniques and Astral Navigation for the Unemployed

Straight Brandy, Personal Hygiene: Social Confidence for the Newly Single

Damn It to Hell, Heavenly Father: Alcohol Abuse and Ecumenical Dialogue

The Hidden Dangers of Bright-Eyed Optimism

Feline Leukemia and Fecal Incontinence

Enter Hamlet, Exit Pamela: Sexual Apartheid and the Plays of Shakespeare

Scientific Instruments, Ceremonial Robes: Bedroom Secrets

Clinical Depression in Postwar Britain

Demonic Possession in Postwar Britain

Postwar Britain: The Prewar Years

How to Get Ahead in Advertising

Source: *New Oxford American Dictionary*

Drugs

The Damnedest Thing

He leapt out of the car just before it was blown apart.
A lumbering bear of a man,
He vaulted cleanly through the open window—
The damnedest thing I ever saw.
He propped himself up on one elbow,
Fanned himself with his hat.
"I've decided to give up drinking."
I helped him up,
Inquired where he lived.
He gave a sudden jerk of his head—
He had trouble keeping his balance.
He asked me for a light,
Mumbled something I didn't catch.
He was talking absolute nonsense.
A crowd gathered on the opposite side of the street.
Shrapnel had penetrated his head and chest.
I felt my pulse quicken.
The ringing of fire alarms.
The still of the night.
I asked him if he had any thoughts on how it had happened.
His big brown eyes were dull and unexpressive.
He nodded vaguely.
He gave a long, weary sigh.

You didn't need x-ray eyes to know what was going on.
He began yawning and looking at his watch.
Then, suddenly, *zoom*! He was off.

Source: *New Oxford American Dictionary*

Diane Smoked Jive

Everyone was out of it in the fifties: cops sitting around drinking, blowing smoke, and kidding; gangbangers making careers of slingin' 'caine. I'd wonder why and do another line, but I never looked at it as if I were some big drug addict.

So Diane smoked jive, pot, and tea. She was twenty-two years old, a real foxy little chick with auburn hair. She wasn't especially smart, but she was built—gams and a pair of maracas that will haunt me in my dreams. Boy, she was smooth. She was moving with a fast bunch of kids who did drugs and played mind games and had group sex and I don't know what else.

I told her I'd make her a star, and she said, "Oh yeah?," all blue-eyed about it. I was showing off, ego-tripping. A small-fry writer like me! I was just about nutty, I was so lonely—a carefree single lesbo looking for love.

Everybody knew she was bound to come unwrapped. She came at me something awful, but I don't take crap from anybody. Not anymore, toots, not anymore, my precious darling angel.

Source: *Dictionary of American Slang*

Duty

The King's Escape

Saved from the gallows by a last-minute reprieve: the story of the king's escape seized the public imagination—"Our most sovereign lord the King! He must have managed to purloin a copy of the key! His diabolical cunning!"

The sacred relic had been hidden away in a sealed cavern where a black yew gloom'd the stagnant air. He faced west and watched the sunset. Traveling across Europe, he hung on to his mount's bridle, alive to the thrill of danger. He traversed the forest, went riding over hill and dale, a grouse moor, an olive grove, a peat bog, a labyrinth of swamps and channels, a featureless landscape of snow and ice, a nest of giant mountains, ground frozen hard as a rock. He sailed 474 miles in one twenty-four-hour burst. He fell prey to loneliness and a wrenching sense of dislocation, mighty beasts, abominable weather, rumors of strange creatures haunting the lake's bottomless nether regions, night people, intolerable levels of hardship. Therewith he rose: a valiant warrior on a single-handed crusade.

He died anyway; so it had all been for nothing. They found his body washed up on the beach. An ill-fated expedition. Eventually the lot fell on the king's daughter.

Sources: *New Oxford American Dictionary*, *Merriam-Webster's Collegiate Dictionary*

Mary and Beth

Beth stood there in the doorway with an impatient scowl, muttering Hail Marys under her breath. The line for tickets was long, and the bar was crowded and noisy. Behind her she could hear men's voices—big talk, unearned privileges. She felt the blood drumming in her ears. The band was warming up.

She saw Mary loitering near the cloakrooms like a tiny hummingbird. She looked wan and bleary-eyed, on the point of leaving. The duffle coat looked incongruous with the black dress she wore underneath, and the heavy studded boots she'd insisted on wearing. She looked down and picked some bits of fluff off her sleeve. Beth threw her a look of encouragement.

Nowadays they moved in different circles of friends. She'd had a hard life. Some people found her hard to take, like black coffee, or a dirty joke, or—

There was a brief flurry of activity in the hall. A stocky guy with a furrowed brow and a protruding bottom lip rested a hand on her shoulder, there was a lot of gesticulation, and she was yelling at him loudly in Bavarian, when—

Mary vanished without a trace.

The crowd was clapping and cheering as Beth ran with a stitch in her side into a hot, airless night.

Sources: *New Oxford American Dictionary, Collins English Dictionary, The American Heritage Dictionary*

Education

Sample Problems: Intermediate Mathematics for Poets

What is the <u>volume</u> of a cube with sides 3 centimeters long, <u>one</u> afternoon in late October, as the sunset <u>tinges</u> the lake with pink?

Solve the <u>quadratic</u> equation $2x^2-3x-6=3$ <u>under</u> several feet of water.

What do you get if you <u>multiply</u> 6 by 9 with <u>gay</u> abandon?

A train runs <u>hourly</u> from 7 a.m. to 8 p.m. at the <u>rate</u> of 60 kilometers an hour. I get up at 6 <u>every day</u>. If the meeting starts

at 9:30 sharp, and the journey takes two hours by train, what are we all doing here?

Find the unknown in the following equations, a horse's mane, a perfect stranger, and a plain brown envelope.

At a latitude of 51° north and a longitude of 2° west, Mary laid a clean square of white toweling carefully on the grass. She was like a child. Careful. Thoughtful. Beautiful. Find the cube root of the result.

The idealism of youth. The inevitability of death. The area of a triangle.

The answer is 280°. The question is not yet decided, one way or the other.

Sources: *New Oxford American Dictionary, Collins COBUILD Primary Learner's Dictionary, Collins English Dictionary, Macquarie Dictionary*

Ego

Bands You Probably Haven't Heard Of

Gastric <u>Atrophy</u>
<u>Mortuary</u> Rituals
The Metric <u>System</u>
The Urethral <u>Meatus</u>
The Everlasting <u>No</u>

The Troops on the Ground Are Cynical

Dave's Untimely Return

Men with Fragile Egos

Special Constable Casey and the Unemployed Baptist Choir

Her Royal Highness and the Prussian Musketry

Blueberry Grunt

Noxious Doctrines

Dangling Modifiers

Tableaux

M'lady

Idiot Florist

Hindquarters

Warmonger

Kind Regards, Creamed Corn

Ingenious Machine

The ABCs of Emergency Heart-Lung Resuscitation

MEET YOU AT THE AIRPORT STOP

Lorenzo the Magnificent and His Purposeless Life

The Church of England

Sources: *New Oxford American Dictionary, Collins English Dictionary, Macquarie Dictionary, The Home Book of Proverbs, Maxims and Familiar Phrases*

So Many People to Thank

"Lastly, I would like to thank my parents; God almighty, my faithful compass (He taught me everything I know); my sweet love, my bride-to-be; my most intimate associates, my companions in misfortune, my friends and loved ones; my big sister; my little brother; my maternal grandfather; the scientific community; the textile industry; the Lord Mayor of Sydney; the

Duchess of Kent and other <u>noble</u> ladies; all those who are <u>young</u> at heart; anyone who fancies <u>themselves</u> as a racing driver; the animal, vegetable, and mineral <u>kingdom</u>s; all of creation—<u>animate</u> and inanimate; and my best <u>mate</u>, Steve. Thank you for <u>having</u> me, thank you for all your support and <u>encourage-ment</u>, thank you for your <u>help</u>, thank you very much <u>indeed</u>."

There was <u>dead</u> silence. Emily <u>read</u> over her notes.

"By the power <u>vest</u>ed in me, I now pronounce you man and wife."

Sources: *New Oxford American Dictionary*, *Collins English Dictionary*, *Macquarie Dictionary*

Employment

Personal Assistant

I am writing in reference to your advertisement for a personal assistant. I'm looking for a full-time job, I'm used to hard work, and I have a strong desire to help people—I worked as a teacher for forty years. I set my alarm clock for seven o'clock every morning, I do yoga twice a week, and I'm learning to swim breaststroke. I don't drink beer, wine, or spirits. I do not chew gum in public. I swear to do everything I can to help you. I can type your essays for you. I'm a fast reader. Do you take sugar in your coffee? I learned to hunt and fish when I was a child. I will either walk or take the bus. My hobbies are music and tennis. I've been singing professionally for ten years, and I like singing hymns. I am a Roman Catholic priest. I called you yesterday, but you were out. You can reach me at this phone number. Please make your decision as soon as possible, as I have nowhere else to go.

Source: *Collins COBUILD Primary Learner's Dictionary*

Your Humble Server

The moon peered from behind dark clouds, and the thunder crashed. The king was throned on a rock. Restored to his proper shape by the magician, he and his myrmidons were ensconced in a bunker, a <u>snug</u> hideout from a giant <u>nebu-lous</u> glow.

A slender man with a mouth full of <u>gold filings</u>, the servant bowed <u>humbly</u> before his master.

"The sacred relic has been <u>hid</u>den away in a sealed cavern."

"<u>Good</u> news. And <u>Father</u> Thames?"

"He has died and now sleeps with his <u>fathers</u>."

"<u>Very</u> good."

A <u>tentative</u> conclusion. An <u>awkward</u> silence.

"Master, what must I do to <u>inherit</u> eternal life?"

"Some coffee would be most <u>acceptable</u>."

Sources: *New Oxford American Dictionary*, *The American Heritage Dictionary*, *Merriam-Webster's Collegiate Dictionary*

Erotica

Some Vast Assemblage

She came into the room, almost completely <u>nude</u>, just a <u>trace</u> of a smile. Her skin glowed in the <u>artificial</u> light. He was dressed in jeans, desert boots, and a big plaid <u>overshirt</u>. He sat back and <u>exhaled</u> deeply. He was <u>weak</u>, but he wasn't a bad man. Just a sad, solitary, <u>inadequate</u> man. He had told his wife he was <u>lunching</u> with a client.

She lay on her back giggling, her hands over her face, one eye twinkling at him through the <u>interstices</u> of her spread fingers. An expression she could not <u>decipher</u> came and went upon his face. He stood up and went to the <u>window</u>.

"I hope we're doing the <u>right</u> thing."

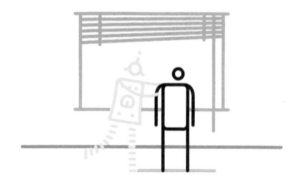

"I wouldn't want to <u>come between</u> husband and wife"—she <u>halt</u>ed in mid-sentence—"but she will probably leave you for a sales <u>droid</u>."

She could see that her remark had <u>hit</u> home. He closed his eyes and <u>sagged</u> against the wall.

"I've made such a <u>mess</u> of my life."

She moved with a sensuous <u>slink</u>. Marianne, with her <u>lush</u> body and provocative green eyes—some vast <u>assemblage</u> of gears and cogs. The girl stood at his <u>side</u>. He saw her lips <u>twitch</u> and her eyelids flutter. The unit was clearly <u>malfunctioning</u>. She dropped her voice to a <u>scratchy</u> whisper.

"Do you <u>love</u> me?"

He hesitated, wondering if there was a <u>trap</u> in the question. He pushed a few <u>stray</u> hairs from her face.

"I love <u>you</u>."

Sources: *New Oxford American Dictionary, Collins COBUILD Primary Learner's Dictionary, The American Heritage Dictionary of Idioms, Macquarie Dictionary*

Escape

Safe House

Please leave a message after the beep.

"Listen to me, I haven't got much time; my flight leaves in less than an hour. You are in a very dangerous situation. Do as I say, or else I won't help you.

"A non-stop flight from London takes you straight to Antigua. There'll be a car waiting for you, a car with foreign number plates. Every church here was named after a saint. It's a high road along a mountain ridge. There is a footbridge that spans the little stream. The house has a large backyard.

"Are you paying attention to what I'm saying? Don't do anything that might cause suspicion. Try learning some relaxation techniques. Get regular exercise. Put on some nice, soothing music. Don't get bored. Keep your brain occupied. Do you understand what I'm telling you, Sean? In this game, there are no rules. Detectives are still searching for the four men. They'll be back in three days. The contact will identify himself simply as Cobra. Be quiet and go to sleep. I'll call you soon."

Sources: *New Oxford American Dictionary, Collins COBUILD Primary Learner's Dictionary*

Young Monarchs

She parted the ferns and looked between them. She had completely forgotten how tired and hungry she was. Her robe trailed along the ground, beaver wool. Running away was not in keeping with her character. She signaled Charlotte to be silent—she trailed behind, whimpering at intervals.

The whole town was heavily fortified: a fast-moving river; a dark, impenetrable forest; a wall of silence. The gates were guarded by uniformed soldiers. A line of watch fires stretched away into the night. The eastern boundary of the wilderness.

They arranged to meet at eleven o'clock. There was still no sign of her. The wind had shifted to the east. There must be something wrong.

Source: *New Oxford American Dictionary*

Exhaustion

Genesis 1 (Reprise)

In the beginning God created the heaven and the earth, artisanal cheeses, the bleakness of winter, Morse code, deviled eggs, erogenous zones, the feeling of fullness you acquire from eating brown rice, gendered occupations, healthy competition, copyright infringement, cherries jubilee, kicky high-heeled boots, lite beer, misshapen fruit, nonsense poetry, oral hygiene, postmodernist theory, quaint country cottages, roller hockey, scented soap, acid trips, unbridled lust, vegetative spores, whitewater rafting, xenophobia, young love, and zippy new sedans. Then he dried up and Phil couldn't get another word out of him.

Sources: *New Oxford American Dictionary, Macquarie Dictionary*

Fame

97-Over Par

The eleventh fairway of a tiny golf course on a hot, airless night. One of the great stars in the American golfing firmament, insensible with drink, was in a bad temper.

"Go to hell!" he spat. It was past midnight.

Socks at half-mast, missing putts that he would normally hole blindfolded, he swore violently under his breath, like an axman at work in a tangled thicket. He was then at the height of his sporting career. He unscrewed the top of a flask and drank the contents.

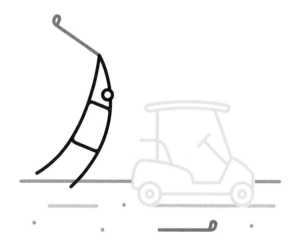

He hit his third shot out of bounds at the 17th. Like a red rag to a bull. His face suddenly turned puce with futile rage, the ball bounced away, and he chased it. He fell with a thud that left him winded.

He lay exhausted and inert, his eyes closed, and with little to distinguish him from one already dead. He lit a cigarette to calm his nerves, and watched the smoke wreathe into the night air.

Sources: *New Oxford American Dictionary*, *Collins English Dictionary*, *Macquarie Dictionary*

Our Descent

The plane shuddered as it entered some turbulence.

"This is the captain speaking. The weather has changed for the worse, so please fasten your seat belts. Well, as I was saying, the more famous I became, the worse I painted. Mass adoration is a highly addictive drug. I was swept along by the crowd, a fantasist with delusions of grandeur. A con artist, painting by numbers. Without Patti to validate my feelings, they seemed not to exist. I was shooting up cocaine, I was drinking copiously, I blew my mind on LSD . . . art in the nineties! When in Rome, you know? The rest, as they say, is history—a big unframed abstract. Self-doubt creeps in, and that swiftly turns to depression, artifice, and outright fakery. We turn to dust, and all our mightiest works die too. It all got too much for me, and I couldn't cope.

"Well, that's enough of me gabbering about myself. I don't want to harp on about the past. It has been an honor to have you. We <u>look</u> forward to seeing you again, and <u>welcome</u> to Washington."

Sources: *New Oxford American Dictionary, Collins COBUILD Primary Learner's Dictionary, Macquarie Dictionary, The Home Book of Proverbs, Maxims, and Familiar Phrases*

Sorry, Wrong Door

He pulled the door <u>to</u> behind him, closed his eyes, and <u>sagged</u> against the wall.

From a hundred <u>throats</u> came the cry "Vive l'Empereur!"

Source: *New Oxford American Dictionary*

Family

Argument Over Jupiter

Laura gave me a sharp <u>push</u>, and I fell to the ground.

"I am <u>sick</u> of all your complaints!"

"Don't be <u>mean</u> to your brother!"

"Whose <u>side</u> are you on?" Shouts and <u>curses</u> came from all directions.

"Stop <u>fighting</u>!" Mum shouted. "<u>Calm</u> down and listen to me: You two are always fighting and <u>making</u> up again. This is the world's largest and most expensive <u>spacecraft</u>, and you are a part of this family, <u>whether</u> you like it or not. You can go <u>if</u> you want—we have *robots* that we could send to the moon."

There was an <u>awkwardly</u> long silence. Harry took a <u>sip</u> of tea. Aunt Mary <u>shuffled</u> the cards. "Now stop crying and <u>pull</u> yourself together."

Source: *Collins COBUILD Primary Learner's Dictionary*

Cousin Madelyn

I've got a sick cousin over Fayetteville <u>way</u>. Her sight's none <u>too</u> good. I <u>rang</u> her this morning. <u>Idle</u> chatter and <u>tall</u> talk about the mysteries of life. She said she missed me something <u>fierce</u>.

Her boyfriend <u>left</u> her for another woman <u>about</u> a year ago, if memory <u>serves</u>. I <u>heard</u> tell that he went out west. Damned if I care. <u>Impertinent</u> boy. She <u>grew</u> her hair long, decided to <u>change</u> her name, moved into that <u>barn</u> of a house. After the accident, she didn't <u>feel</u> up to driving, so she took to her room and was not at <u>home</u> to friends.

I didn't like it, and I told her <u>so</u>. People who live in a <u>vacuum</u> so that the world outside them is of no moment. <u>Bad</u> news.

It was easier in the <u>old</u> days. We used to <u>go</u> hunting, we <u>done</u> a lot of rodeoin'—we had a good <u>time</u>. A child's <u>idea</u> of time. We were always within <u>sound</u> of the train whistles, the <u>low</u>ing of cattle, the <u>distant</u> bark of some farm dog, the spit and <u>hiss</u> of a cornered cat, tunes in waltz <u>time</u> . . . Animals in close confinement. I will <u>never</u>, ever forget it.

Life <u>goes on</u>. I'd better give her a <u>ring</u> tomorrow.

Sources: *New Oxford American Dictionary, Macquarie Dictionary, Merriam-Webster's Collegiate Dictionary*

Fantasies

Barbara

The whole world seemed to be sleeping, apart from Barbara. She found herself in bed in a strange place—a research station in the rain forest, a bird sanctuary—abandoning herself to moony fantasies: a research biologist with impeccable credentials had been fingered for team leader, and she had been deputed to look after him while Clarissa was away. He had charm, good looks, and an amusing insouciance; she had a thing about men who wore glasses, men of culture, men with passions unruled. She had had plenty of flirtations—now she had fallen in love. Color bloomed in her cheeks. He leaned forward to take her hand. She looked down, terrified that he would read fear on her face—

A sudden sound in the doorway startled her. A shiver shook her slim frame. She lodged this idea in the back of her mind for future reference.

Source: *New Oxford American Dictionary*

To Do

- Get groceries.
- Do the dishes.
- Call the doctor.

- <u>Take</u> down the Christmas tree.
- <u>Make</u> like you're happy.
- Pick yourself up and <u>dust</u> yourself off.
- <u>Forget</u> all this romantic stuff.
- Stop your <u>theatrics</u>.
- Put some <u>padding</u> in the résumé.
- Improve your golf <u>swing</u>.
- Get down off your <u>high</u> horse.
- Return this dog to its <u>rightful</u> owner.
- Start <u>afresh</u>.
- <u>Grow</u> a beard.
- <u>Take</u> up mountain climbing.
- Learn more about <u>pesticide-free</u> gardening.
- <u>Put</u> a little money aside, travel to <u>far-distant</u> lands, an <u>uncontaminated</u> island paradise, and <u>start</u> a business. <u>Raise</u> cattle. <u>Raise</u> corn and soybeans. <u>Living</u> on rice and fish, <u>establish</u> goodwill in the neighborhood, <u>make</u> friends, sit and <u>listen</u> to the radio, and be at <u>ease</u>.

Sources: *New Oxford American Dictionary*, *Macquarie Dictionary*, *The American Heritage Dictionary*

Forgetfulness

July 8

I found an English garden all about me—
Peach trees in blossom,
Cut grass,
A cheerful disposition of colors and textures.
A sigh escaped my lips.
I heard a sound and froze in my tracks,
Wriggled through a gap in the fence.
Here goes . . . !
Had an impulse to run away.
A plan of action finally jelled in my mind:
keep quiet.
I had to laugh when I saw who my opponent was:
a cat with a monotone coat.
All that trouble for nothing.
I ate one peach,
Paused to clear my throat, then proceeded,
Life being very short, and the quiet hours of it few.
Then I remembered that today is your birthday.
Sniffed the lilacs,
Took a deep breath—
Moist, cool, soft grass growing underfoot,
Dusk verging into night.
I see what seems to be a dead tree—

<u>Xylophagous</u> fungi.

<u>You</u> can't win them all.

Today I accomplished <u>zero</u>.

Source: *The American Heritage Dictionary*

Forgiveness

Confessional

What grieves you, my son?

Pray for me, Father! I am a sinful man. I'm eaten up with guilt. I have a list of vices as long as your arm.

I'm sick of this town. I'm estranged from my son. I slashed the tires of his van, and I felt nothing. I don't eat breakfast. I'm afraid of dogs. I always peer at other people's shopping carts as we stand in line. I went to a few parties and had a good time. I stayed out late at the blues club and came home blootered. I stole a small fishing boat and sailed it to the Delta, and I'd do it again in a heartbeat.

I started drinking again after six years of abstinence. I've put on nearly a stone since September. I'm desperate for a cigarette. I believe in ghosts. I conned David into giving me your home number. My watch has stopped. My rent check bounced. I burned myself on the stove. I don't know a great deal about politics. I didn't get into Nirvana until after *MTV Unplugged* came out—I'm always late to the party.

I don't want to take up any more of your time. I want to get stinking drunk and forget. I'm going to lie down. Please forgive me these things and the people I have wronged. If anyone finds out, you're dead meat.

Sources: *New Oxford American Dictionary*, *Collins English Dictionary*

Furniture

Instructions for Assembly

1. Take a square of sandpaper, <u>rough</u> side out.
2. <u>Sand</u> the rusty areas until you expose bare metal.
3. You can't <u>hold</u> yourself responsible for what happened.

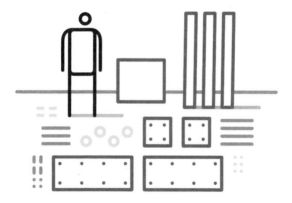

4. Smooth over with a cloth, <u>apply</u>ing even pressure.
5. <u>Drill</u> holes through the tiles for the masonry pins.
6. The inquiry <u>blamed</u> the engineer for the accident.
7. <u>Screw</u> the hinge to your new door.

8. Ensure that the baseboard is straight and <u>plumb</u>.

9. It was *his* <u>fault</u> she had died.

10. <u>Nail</u> the edge framing to the wall.

Source: *New Oxford American Dictionary*

Games

Check

The house is <u>ablaze</u>, police <u>set</u> up a roadblock on Tenth Street, <u>thirty</u> were hurt, <u>forty</u> were arrested, and Neil is still <u>recovering</u> from shock. <u>Once</u> more, you've proven yourself inept at chess.

Sources: *New Oxford American Dictionary, The American Heritage Dictionary*

How to Play

The house rules are <u>crystal</u> clear, don't look <u>so</u> worried. The game is <u>structured</u> so that there are five ways to win. Each player is given eight wooden <u>meeples</u>, a snooker <u>cue</u>, a <u>set</u> of false teeth, and a <u>pneumatic</u> drill. The best <u>play</u> is to lead with the three of clubs. If Black <u>moves</u> his bishop, he loses a pawn, two red aces, and a <u>stiff</u> club. <u>Roll</u> a two, three, or twelve. Move your <u>counter</u> one square for each spot on the dice. You can't move a <u>meeple</u> over a bridge unless a meeple is on the bridge—that <u>move</u> will put your king in check. If a <u>batter</u> hits a bunt foul with two strikes, he is out. <u>Shuffle</u> the deck, add the numbers together, and <u>take</u> away five. <u>Aim</u> for the middle of the target. Each correct answer <u>scores</u> ten points, and red aces <u>score</u> twenty. Anyone shooting a hole in one must <u>shout</u> for all players on the course. The rules state <u>categorically</u>, "No violence," but the magician *may* cast a <u>spell</u> on himself. There are hundreds of prizes to be <u>won</u>, and the <u>umpire</u>'s decision is final. May the Lord have <u>mercy</u> on your soul.

Sources: *New Oxford American Dictionary*, *Collins COBUILD Primary Learner's Dictionary*, *Collins English Dictionary*

Gossip

A Brief Conversation between Two Friends Who Are Also Lions

"Have I got some <u>hot</u> gossip for you! Joanna had a <u>tiff</u> with her boyfriend, so <u>Todd</u> tried to set her up with one of his friends, and between you and me, I think he's had some <u>work</u> done. He must be seventy if he's a <u>day</u>."

Shirley <u>roar</u>ed in amusement.

Sources: *New Oxford American Dictionary*, *Macquarie Dictionary*

Grief

Early Drafts of the Five Stages of Grief

- Denial, Profanity, Alcoholism, Darkness, Lunacy
- Fighting, Sullen silence, Fighting, Cold reason, Caffeine
- Righteous indignation, Mindless violence, Strong language, Resigned acceptance, Ice skating
- Sadness, Sadness, Sadness, Sadness, Solitude
- Archery, Bakery, Pottery, Bravery, Scenery
- Temptation, Contrition, Scripture, Communion, A seven-day trip for two to Hawaii
- A stubborn resistance, A melancholy mood, An absence of several weeks, A gentle wind, A suspicion of a smile

---

Sources: *New Oxford American Dictionary*, *Macquarie Dictionary*

Good Grief

Cathy stared into vacancy, seeing nothing. Her hair was a tumble of untamed curls. Her nose was blobbed with paint. She was wrapped in thought. She puzzled over the squiggles and curves on the paper. Seventeen years later, and she still had the moment filed away in her memory.

She lived in a Podunk town notable for nothing except

the girls' school where she taught art, a stretch of road between nowhere and <u>nowhere</u>. A post <u>office</u>, a <u>DIY</u> store, the tavern just a <u>joint</u> with Formica tables, a vinyl floor, lights over the mirrors. She had been brought up in a family where she felt <u>unappreciated</u> and undervalued. Her father was a <u>tyrant</u> and a bully, and there was a powerful <u>strain</u> of insanity on her mother's side of the family. She followed her brother's <u>example</u> and deserted her family, like a pilot <u>jettison</u>ing aircraft fuel. She <u>commit</u>ted herself to her art, <u>gave</u> herself up to her work. She saw herself as <u>neither</u> wife nor mother—she didn't need to <u>measure</u> herself against some ideal.

She would always remember the <u>moment</u> they met: a <u>chance</u> encounter by a <u>dumpy</u> little diner with a CLOSED sign hanging in the window, a <u>dirty</u> joke. Their faces <u>lit up</u>, and one dug the other in the ribs. They became friends in the <u>course</u> of their long walks, their <u>world-weary</u> cynical talk. Their <u>admiration</u> for each other was genuine.

It was a <u>miracle</u> that more people hadn't been killed or injured. Two buildings collapsed, trapping scores of people in the <u>rubble</u>. Through <u>broken</u> sobs, she stared at the card as if she could contact its writer by <u>clairvoyance</u>. Her faithful <u>shadow</u>, a Yorkshire terrier called Heathcliff, <u>appraised</u> himself in the mirror and <u>grunt</u>ed his thanks as she stroked his <u>furrow</u>ed brow. The dog <u>nuzzle</u>d up against her.

She <u>swallow</u>ed hard, sniffing back her tears. Her body was <u>striped</u> with bands of sunlight.

Sources: *New Oxford American Dictionary, Collins English Dictionary, The American Heritage Dictionary*

My Apologies

Sorry, am I <u>disturbing</u> you? I apologize for coming over unannounced <u>like</u> this. Sorry to <u>trouble</u> you. Sorry to <u>barge</u> in on your cozy evening.

The <u>main</u> reason I came today was to say sorry.

I'm sorry, Susan, I <u>screwed</u> up. I'm sorry, I <u>totally</u> didn't mean it. I'm sorry I <u>blew up</u> at you, I'm sorry. I behaved <u>stupidly</u>, I'm sorry if I <u>offended</u> you. I'm sorry, but I just had to <u>get a load off my mind</u>.

<u>Look</u>, I'm sorry, I didn't mean it. I'm sorry! I'll do better! <u>Give me a break!</u>

Sorry, I didn't mean to <u>snap</u> at you.

Believe me, Susan, I am <u>truly</u> sorry. I'm <u>terribly</u> sorry. I'm <u>frightfully</u> sorry. I'm <u>dreadfully</u> sorry. I told him I never wanted to see him again, but I didn't expect him to take it <u>literally</u>. I'm <u>sorry</u> he's gone.

I'm sorry, but <u>there it is</u>. I ask you to <u>find</u> it in your heart to forgive me.

Sources: *New Oxford American Dictionary, Collins COBUILD Primary Learner's Dictionary, The American Heritage Dictionary of Idioms, NTC's Dictionary of British Slang*

Hh

Hallucination

Cabin Fever Dream

We were <u>face to face</u> with death during the avalanche. The storm moved in <u>fast and furious</u>, the lights <u>flickered</u>, and suddenly it was dark. The snow was so heavy, we feared the roof would <u>fall in</u>. Now we've been snowed in for a week, and everyone has <u>cabin fever</u>. We're <u>out of</u> sugar and coffee. Someone's used <u>all</u> the milk. Our supplies have <u>run out</u>. I'm <u>dying</u> for some fresh air.

I thought I saw my father, but I must have been <u>seeing things</u>; he died twenty years ago. He was playing <u>chess</u> with his uncle. He was dressed in <u>white</u> from head to toe. When he saw me, he <u>smiled</u>. I asked him <u>when</u> he was coming back, I asked him but he didn't <u>answer</u>. He just dropped two sugar <u>cubes</u> into his coffee, and blew on his hands to <u>warm</u> them up.

Sources: *Collins COBUILD Primary Learner's Dictionary*, *The American Heritage Dictionary of Idioms*

Health

Breakup Side Effects

Dullness of vision

Heaviness of heart

Declarations of love

A paroxysm of weeping

Increased shallowness of breath

Traces of acid

Extremes of temperature

Aggressive behavior

Criminal tendencies

Kleptomania

Pyromania

Alcoholism

Hedonism

Barbarism

Greasy skin

Bad headaches

Debilitating back pain

Economy of words

Resigned acceptance

Voyages of exploration

Vows of chastity

Shortness of memory

Source: *New Oxford American Dictionary*

History

Haunting the Docents

I lived here years ago, when men wore frills and finery and let their hair grow into long lovelocks, before the queen's fair name was breathed upon, before the war.

The castle was built as protection against the Saxons—a fortress high up on a hill, the lofty battlements thickly enwreathed with ivy. The moon glimmered through the mist, and the minstrels sang of courtly love to the king and his people: a wondrous assemblage of noble knights, cruel temptresses, and impossible loves.

Today, the castle has more than 650,000 visitors a year. And I am returned, an echo of the past, a phantom who haunts lonely roads, an incongruous figure among the tourists.

Our tour guide is *very* knowledgeable and entertaining—

"The king was tricked out of his land." You don't know the half of it.

"He was reputed to have the finest French table of the time!" Is that so?

"It is said the king died a violent death!" I hardly think so. The bells tolled the queen's death, and he jumped from the window into the moat below. It was done. After her death, he felt that his life was meaningless. He said so himself: "The moon itself is dead."

The heir to the <u>throne</u>, on a <u>guided</u> tour of the castle. <u>What</u> luck.

Want to see the library? It's really <u>something</u>.

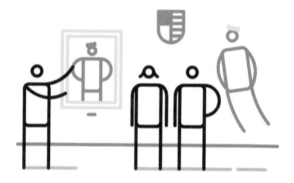

Sources: *New Oxford American Dictionary, Collins COBUILD Primary Learner's Dictionary, Collins English Dictionary, Macquarie Dictionary*

Horror

Absolute Certainty

Teresa paled in the <u>half-light</u> of the passage. She had heard an insistent voice <u>calling</u> her name, a voice <u>touched</u> by hysteria. She <u>stood</u> still, heart hammering. She was <u>alone</u> that evening.

Someone was <u>coming</u>, and she knew with absolute <u>certainty</u> that they were dead.

The entire house was plunged into pitch <u>blackness</u>. She felt her throat <u>close</u> up. She tried to laugh, an attempt hurriedly abandoned because she could feel that it was a nervous laughter that might turn to weeping—dreadful, <u>hysterical</u> weeping that one couldn't control. She <u>felt</u> the presence of a stranger in the room. Horror came over her in <u>waves</u>. Two <u>soulless</u> black eyes were watching her.

What happened next was a <u>phantasmagoria</u> of horror and mystery. But I can't stand around <u>chitchat</u>ting. There's blood caked an inch thick on the walls, and until we clean up and lay down the new carpet, it's going to look a little <u>rough</u> around the edges.

Sources: *New Oxford American Dictionary, Collins English Dictionary, Macquarie Dictionary*

Silver Birches

The guesthouse was <u>erected</u> in the eighteenth century, <u>half</u>-hidden in the trees like a reclusive, <u>timorous</u> creature. I took the job with the <u>idea</u> of getting some money together, but now I felt decidedly off. It was <u>outside</u> my experience and beyond my ability. As he turned the <u>brights</u> on and we drove along the dirt road, a flash of lightning <u>illuminated</u> the house. It was obvious that something had gone <u>adrift</u>. A <u>flicker</u> of movement caught my eye: A <u>misty</u>, out-of-focus silhouette. A fiend in human <u>shape</u>. Peter <u>swore</u> under his breath.

The door was wide <u>open</u>. We walked <u>inside</u>, and I suddenly felt <u>desolate</u> and bereft. The <u>wind</u> howled about the building. Rivulets of water coursed down the panes, <u>puddling</u> on the sill. He swung his flashlight in a wide <u>arc</u>, and all at <u>once</u> the noise stopped. I felt the sting of the cold, <u>bitter</u> air. A profound loneliness, an <u>oppressive</u> emptiness.

It wasn't until I saw the photograph that everything <u>clicked</u> into place. It was <u>clear</u> that we were in a trap.

The <u>creak</u> of a floorboard broke the silence, a voice high in pitch but rich in <u>timbre</u>: *The time is <u>approaching</u> when you will be destroyed. He <u>sleeps</u> beneath the silver birches. He <u>sleeps</u> beneath the silver birches. He <u>sleeps</u> beneath the silver birch—*

Sources: *New Oxford American Dictionary, Collins English Dictionary*

What He Is

He is, in <u>brief</u>, the embodiment of evil. He's a deeply <u>sick</u> man from whom society needs to be protected. He's an egotistical, <u>mean-spirited</u>, abusive man. He's a <u>lying</u>, cheating snake in the grass. He's a treacherous, <u>brain-damaged</u> old vulture. He's emerged as a racist and an <u>anti-feminist</u>. He's a self-absorbed <u>egotist</u>. He's a blackmailer and an <u>extortionist</u>. He's a shameless publicity-<u>seeker</u>. He's <u>arrogant</u> and opinionated. He's lazy and <u>unreliable</u>. He's all <u>talk</u>. He's a <u>bumbling</u> fool. He's a real <u>character</u>. He's a bit of a <u>womanizer</u>. He's by no means the only senior politician who has mislaid his <u>moral compass</u>. He's being unfairly <u>gang</u>ed up on. He's as <u>devious</u> as a politician needs to be. He is shrewder than his <u>disparagers</u> would credit. He's a good guy at <u>heart</u>. He's a very strong leader, very <u>presidential</u> in his performance. He's the <u>ideas man</u>, and the others do the day-to-day work. He's very much a man of the <u>people</u>. After a while, <u>you</u> get used to it.

Source: *New Oxford American Dictionary*

Hospice

Roses

He looked very frail in his hospital bed. There was no fight left in him; he wasn't even capable of standing up. This didn't seem fair to me. He was a painter and a poet. He was a senior naval officer. He was a keen gardener, winning many prizes for his efforts.

The room was small and quiet, with a window that opened outward to an enclosed back garden with a shaped lawn. We watched a squirrel negotiate the topmost branches of a nearby tree, and a woman all in brown—she was crouching over some flower bed.

"It's the wrong time of year for planting roses."

I just said the first thing that came into my head. His face crinkled up in a smile, and he gave me a sly, conspiratorial wink—*is that so?*

Sources: *New Oxford American Dictionary, Collins COBUILD Primary Learner's Dictionary*

Ii

Identity

Noir I

I walked along Broadway, deserted but for the occasional cab, drenched in a harsh white neon light. My feet were sore and my head ached. The place stank like a sewer. I shouldered my way to the bar. Ernie was making out with Bernice. Those kinds of animals ought to be left in the wild. I caught Rhoda's eye and gave her a friendly wave. She's got class—she looks like a princess. I always was a sucker for a good fairy tale.

I was to meet him at 6:30. When we first met, he was a pistol, full of ideals and a natural leader. He was the hot young piano prospect in jazz. Later, at the club, he got tight on brandy, a shot rang out—he claims he was framed. As soon as he got put under pressure, he sang like a canary. Somehow I managed to get the job done: he was paroled after serving nine months of a two-year sentence.

He arrived late. He winked at Nicole as he passed. High-heeled shoes, a platinum wig. The dress didn't suit him.

"I might have known it was you."

"I'm quite a good actress, I suppose. Here's the money I promised you."

"Say, did you notice any blood?"

"What an unfeeling little brute you are."

Source: *New Oxford American Dictionary*

Identity, Mistaken

A Fistful of Feathers

It was <u>late</u> in the afternoon when they drove across the <u>border</u>. The horses were <u>lame</u> and the men were tired.

The village was a <u>settlement</u> of just fifty houses. The church was in <u>ruins</u>, and a girl was sitting on the bottom step.

"Excuse me, <u>ma'am</u>. Where is Mr. Hernandez?"

She looked up for a minute and then <u>continued</u> drawing. The men were carrying knives and <u>clubs</u>.

"He's sitting over <u>there</u>." She pointed to a black bird with a yellow <u>beak</u>. The bird flapped its <u>wings</u>.

"Thank you, <u>darling</u>."

They walked <u>away</u> from the church in silence.

"There must be <u>some</u> mistake."

A <u>cloud</u> of black smoke spread across the sky. Griego felt the cold <u>point</u> of a knife against his neck.

Sources: *New Oxford American Dictionary, Collins COBUILD Primary Learner's Dictionary*

Indigestion

All You Can Eat

The waitress asked, "Are you ready to order?"

"Very much so. I'll have the salad plate, the dish of the day, the seared chicken livers with sautéed potatoes, the braised veal, the stir-fried beef, beef casserole, chicken à la king, lobster bordelaise, roast turkey with all the trimmings, beef and lamb en brochette, the deep-fried onion rings, a bowl of tomato soup—"

"Can I borrow a pen, please?"

He took a pen from his pocket.

"I'll have the seafood platter served on a bed of lettuce; the tagliatelle tossed with guanciale, red onion, olives, and pickled peppers; the sun-dried-tomato-and-mozzarella arancini served with salad; the white pizza topped with rosemary, garlic, anchovies, and black olives; the roast duck with jalapeño jelly; the crab and avocado salad; the grilled fish; chicken cacciatore; chicken dhansak; chicken marsala; chicken piccata; chicken supreme; the vegetable soup—"

"You have to try the chicken and ham croquetas—"

"Very good. Oh, I've lost my place." He paused in perplexity.

"The vegetable soup . . ."

"Ah! The vegetable soup, a bunch of bananas, a cheese-and-pickle sandwich, a loaf of bread, a bowl of cereal, a dish of oysters, tuna sashimi, clam chowder, jugged hare, spit-roasted lamb, pickled onions, baked apples, stewed apples, candied yams, creamed turnips, jellied eels, brined anchovies, dry-roasted peanuts, baby carrots, new potatoes, cocktail sausages, raw eggs, deviled eggs, chocolate eggs, tortilla chips dipped in salsa, a shake and a regular fries, an apple dipped in caramel, lashings of cream, the blackberry-and-apricot parfait, the finest cheese in all the land, all of the cake, steamed milk with a shot of espresso, some digestive mints, and a strawberry margarita, but hold the tequila. I like my steak medium rare, and I like lamb well done."

"Is that all?"

"Is there a doctor in the house?"

"Five ambulances are on standby."

"Very good."

Sources: *New Oxford American Dictionary, Collins COBUILD Primary Learner's Dictionary, Collins English Dictionary, Macquarie Dictionary, The American Heritage Dictionary, Merriam-Webster's Collegiate Dictionary*

Inheritance

Mother Lode

Howard stood in the <u>middle</u> of the room like a partially <u>inflated</u> balloon. Wearing a jacket that was too <u>tight</u> for him, he thrust his hands in his pockets, <u>hunch</u>ing his shoulders. The house was in a <u>mess</u>. <u>Blank</u> cassettes, paperback <u>original</u>s, a suit of <u>armor</u> . . . The <u>remains</u> of a sandwich lunch were on the table. He lit a cigarette to <u>calm</u> his nerves.

A suit of <u>armor</u>?

His mother's small estate had <u>pass</u>ed to him after her death. A large white house falling into gentle <u>ruin</u>, huddled against the white <u>immensities</u> of land and sky—one of those lonely New England farmhouses that make the landscape lonelier. There was a <u>fungus</u> of outbuildings behind the house, a pond two miles <u>around</u>. There was damage to the house's <u>external</u> walls, and a hole <u>gaped</u> in the roof. It took three hours and several bus <u>transfers</u> to get there.

He went around the office <u>collecting</u> old coffee cups, riffling through the <u>papers</u> on her desk. The light <u>percolating</u> through the stained-glass windows cast colored patterns on the floor, on deep-pile carpet that <u>lapped</u> against his ankles. He sat on the <u>bottom</u> of an upturned bucket and looked around <u>desperately</u>.

Sources: *New Oxford American Dictionary*, *Collins COBUILD Primary Learner's Dictionary*, *Collins English Dictionary*, *The American Heritage Dictionary*

Interrogation

The Night in Question

An imposing seventeenth-century manor house in the howling wilderness. Outside, the wind was as wild as ever. Inside, an enrapt audience sat bolt upright, in the hands of malignant fate.

Lord Derby, the tycoon for whom money was no object; Lady Caroline Lamb, the domineering matriarch; Master James Williams, the sophisticated metropolitan; Mrs. Sally Jones, the acclaimed artist and accomplished pianist; Mr. Robert Smith, the house servant. A very crowded room.

They were sitting around the hearth, their faces blanched with fear. In the shadow where the balcony overhangs, a man was leaning against the wall. Detective Sergeant Fox. A man of precise military bearing. A man of dignity and unbending principle. A man who had known better times. His face glowed in the dull lamplight. Through the steady thrum of rain on the windows, his soft Scottish burr:

"Lord Derby, where were you on the night when the murder took place?"

He cast his mind back to the fatal evening.

"I was aboard the *St. Roch*, shortly before she sailed for the Northwest Passage."

"When did you get home?"

"It was actually about an hour after moonrise." The fire suddenly crackled and spat sparks.

"Do you really expect me to believe that?"

"Whatever do you mean? Where is this argument leading? Why are you taxing me with these preposterous allegations?"

The sergeant lifted an admonitory finger. "The body of evidence is too substantial to disregard."

"I'm sure there's a perfectly rational explanation."

"Aye, you're right about that."

"You think I perhaps killed Westbourne, yes?" His voice was rough with barely suppressed fury. Everybody was listening intently.

"In the prime of life. The poor bastard." The thunder crashed, and wind whistled through the cracks in the windows.

"You're asking for trouble, you filthy beast."

"You miserable old creep." Attraction and antagonism were crackling between them.

"Go to hell!" he spat.

"Go and drown yourself!"

"I love you!"

"I love you!"

The two embraced, holding each other tightly.

Sources: *New Oxford American Dictionary*, *Macquarie Dictionary*, *The American Heritage Dictionary*, *The Home Book of Proverbs, Maxims and Familiar Phrases*

William

I was in love once. He was a pleasant boy, if a poor timekeeper. Of noble birth, between you and me. Shockingly bad manners. He wasn't handsome in the accepted sense—he wasn't exactly ugly, but he wasn't an oil painting either. I'd known him for many years, since I was seventeen. He was awkward and nervous around girls—a being from outer space, with his hands buried in the pockets of his overcoat. I couldn't take my eyes off him.

We had a good time. We were fresh out of art school. We took the night train to Scotland, two suitcases flung anyhow. We lived together off and on. Everything mattered intensely to William, and he made it plain what he wanted from me. He profoundly altered the whole course of my life. Then he just vanished into thin air.

He had started messing with drugs, but none of it meant anything to him. He seemed more content, less bitter. I never saw any signs, but then again, maybe I wasn't looking.

Now do you understand why I want to leave the past behind me? For Chrissake, listen to me! You are living in a fantasy <u>land</u>! I <u>swear</u> by all I hold dear that I had nothing to do with it!

Can we <u>move on</u> to the next question?

Sources: *New Oxford American Dictionary*, *Collins English Dictionary*

Jealousy

John and Victor (and Catherine)

"Ladies and gentlemen, your attention, please. First of all, I'd like to thank you for coming. Will you see to it that your glasses are charged? It's been such a terrific day—many thanks to all concerned.

My name is John, and Victor and I go back longer than I care to admit. Fraternity brothers in the balmy days of late summer, tomcatting all night and sleeping all afternoon. Filthy language, floodlit football fields . . . Some of the best times in my life. Perhaps that summer will mark the high spot in my life.

I know Catherine will pardon me. Look, lady, I was ahead of you in line. I have nothing against you personally, but it's thanks to you that he's in this mess.

Come on, let's get it over with. I hereby propose a toast to the bride and groom. If that's your final decision, I guess that's that. Don't come crawling back to me later when you realize your mistake. Now, if you'll excuse me, I am going to get diabolically drunk."

Sources: *New Oxford American Dictionary*, *Collins COBUILD Primary Learner's Dictionary*, *The American Heritage Dictionary*

Toby

"I was in this store when who <u>should</u> I see across the street but Toby. He was obviously stoned out of his <u>gourd</u>—he didn't <u>understand</u> a word I said. He was ogling the girls, looking for a little <u>action</u>. There's been a <u>rumor mill</u> on him for years. I <u>know</u> for a fact that he can't speak a word of Japanese. He thinks he's real <u>hot shit</u>—his ego is <u>big enough to choke a horse</u>. He tried repeatedly to <u>bring</u> up the subject of marriage, so I <u>told</u> him what he could do with his diamond, to <u>hell</u> with the consequences. I told the <u>son of a bitch</u> what I thought of him.

"I don't want to <u>harp</u> on about the past, but <u>sparks</u> always fly when you two get together, and I don't like him <u>at all</u>. He <u>still</u> lives with his mother, and his smile <u>gives me the creeps</u>. I don't want him <u>meddling</u> in our affairs. I got up and <u>took care of business</u>, so let's just <u>wipe the slate clean</u> and pretend it never happened. Please pass <u>the</u> asparagus."

Sources: *New Oxford American Dictionary, Dictionary of American Slang*

Judgment

The Accused

At six feet, six inches, he was an <u>arresting</u> figure. His deep voice was laced with a hint of an <u>Alabaman</u> accent, and dressed <u>all</u> in black, he had an <u>animal magnetism</u> that women found irresistible. An <u>austere</u> man with a rigidly puritanical outlook, he had no <u>academic</u> qualifications, but he was the only <u>able-bodied</u> man on the farm. He <u>adored</u> his mother.

His wife's death had long been the subject of rumor and <u>anecdote</u>. Some loved her, some hated her, few were <u>ambivalent</u> about her. He read the letter <u>aloud</u>. His address was <u>abrupt</u> and uneremonious, and his voice was calm and <u>authoritative</u>. He <u>accepted</u> that he had made a mistake—problems like these should not occur, but <u>accidents</u> do happen.

He smoothed his hair and <u>adjusted</u> his tie.

Source: *New Oxford American Dictionary*

Justice

Another Animated Description of Mr. Maps

The police have arrested a <u>suspect</u>.

He has piercing blue <u>eyes</u> and a <u>mass</u> of curly hair. A man of short stature, he was born and <u>raised</u> in San Francisco. He is an <u>only</u> child, an <u>avid</u> reader of science fiction, and a man of <u>unusual</u> talent. A lab technician <u>skilled</u> in electronics, he <u>fancies</u> himself an amateur psychologist, a <u>talented</u> young musician, and an art <u>collector</u>. He is a man of <u>private means</u>. He is a fluent English and French <u>speaker</u>. He does not lack perception or native <u>wit</u>. He is a great <u>lover</u> of cats and a celebrated <u>patron</u> of the arts. A man of <u>cultivation</u> and taste. It gives him pleasure to keep things shipshape and <u>Bristol fashion</u>. He was elected a <u>fellow</u> of the Geological Society. He was <u>named</u> to head a joint UN–OAS diplomatic effort. He's a pretentious <u>son</u> of a gun, but he's got a heart of gold. He is a good, <u>righteous</u> man, I am sure.

The <u>jury</u> returned unanimous guilty verdicts.

Source: *New Oxford American Dictionary*

Karma

Apples

I was <u>eager</u> for it, <u>anxious</u> to please like a dog with ears <u>erect</u>. She stood in the doorway, resplendent in her <u>gaudery</u>. The <u>waist</u> of a violin, the <u>poise</u> of a bird in the air. She seemed to <u>illumine</u> the space around her.

The air was <u>heavy</u> with the sweet odor of apples. There was certainty and uncertainty, and most of all a sense of hurtling <u>willy-nilly</u> into something so extraordinary, so risky, and so filled with a potential of pain for me that for an impulsive instant I wanted to turn around and run for my life. My skin <u>goosepimpled</u> at the thought. My face <u>crimsoned</u>, and my hands began to shake.

<u>If</u> only I had known.

She took three <u>paces</u> across the room with <u>feline</u> softness of step, when the room went <u>dark</u>. The temperature <u>fell</u> ten degrees. <u>Dead</u> silence. <u>Circumambient</u> gloom. The <u>whirr</u> of wings. She spoke quietly, <u>as</u> to herself: "Thou shalt have <u>none</u> other gods before me. I have watched you do things I confess I could never <u>condone</u>. I will not <u>pardon</u> your transgressions."

I felt my throat constrict, a <u>feeling</u> of fear, a <u>feeling</u> of sorrow, and a <u>feeling</u> of warmth, pain, and drowsiness.

Source: *Macquarie Dictionary*

Fantasy Adolescent

Ben <u>shuffled</u> his feet in the awkward silence. The fire had <u>singed</u> his eyebrows.

"How often must I <u>beat</u> it into your head that dragons are dangerous?"

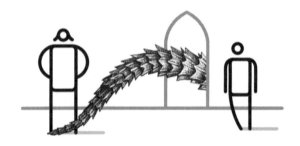

Sources: *New Oxford American Dictionary, Dictionary of American Slang*

Ketamine

Straight from the Horse's Mouth

Do you <u>mind</u> if I open a window?

It's too hot in <u>here</u>. I feel really tired all of a <u>sudden</u>.

My skin feels <u>prickly</u>, I feel like I'm wearing a cloak of <u>invisibility</u>.

Wait a <u>minute</u>, something is wrong here, I'm not feeling <u>well</u>, I'd <u>like</u> to go home, <u>chill</u> out, okay, <u>everything</u> is going okay. <u>Everything</u> is going okay, keep calm and don't <u>raise</u> your voice, <u>who</u>'s there what was your name <u>again</u> what are you doing here <u>anyway</u> what <u>shall</u> we do now what are we all doing <u>here</u> how <u>wide</u> do you think this house is <u>have</u> we got enough chairs is the one-dollar bill the only <u>banknote</u> with George Washington's picture on it what's the <u>matter</u> don't come <u>near</u> me I'm going <u>to</u> lie down do you <u>mind</u> if I open a window all the puppets came to <u>life</u> again

---

Sources: *New Oxford American Dictionary*, *Collins COBUILD Primary Learner's Dictionary*, *Collins English Dictionary*

Kidnapping

Corsican Coast Interrogation

He sat feeling old and beaten. His eyes were open, but he could see nothing.

He was picked up by a frigate after ditching his plane in the Mediterranean—he had flown to open sea, put the plane in a nosedive, and ejected. Now his hands were manacled behind his back, his body temperature was high, and he had become dehydrated. He was trying to clear the phantoms from his head and grasp reality, when there was a shuffle of approaching feet.

"Who's there?"

He shifted a little in his chair.

"Do you have a client named Pedersen?" Like the voice of a teacher talking to a rather dull child.

"I don't know what you mean."

"Who has the key to the safe? Who is the woman in the red dress?"

"I don't know what you mean!" He heard the smash of glass.

"What do you want!"

He blinked, momentarily blinded by a pinpoint of light from a flashlight.

"Cenzo, you old rogue!"

"Good lord, Jack Stone, as I live and breathe!"

"Well, I didn't expect to see you here! What have you been up to, you old bugger?"

"Oh, love, life, and all that jazz. You're looking swell!"

"I've been on the 5:2 diet for seven weeks!"

"I'll be damned!"

There were several moments of awkward silence. The ship pitched and rolled.

"Well, this is a pretty state of affairs to have gotten into."

Sources: *New Oxford American Dictionary, Collins COBUILD Primary Learner's Dictionary, Collins English Dictionary, Dictionary of American Slang, Merriam-Webster's Collegiate Dictionary*

Language

Very Good Boy

"Does your dog do any tricks?"

"He published his autobiography last autumn."

Laura's brow wrinkled.

"I beg your pardon?"

"He wrote a book on the history of Russian ballet, and he has a novel in the works too—a spy novel set in Berlin. He needed something both to challenge his skills and to regain his crown as the king of the thriller."

She looked down at the chocolate-colored Labrador, and gave David a look of complete incomprehension.

"He's the strong, <u>silent</u> type."

The dog licked <u>its</u> paw.

"Down, <u>boy</u>, down."

Sources: *New Oxford American Dictionary, Collins COBUILD Primary Learner's Dictionary, The American Heritage Dictionary, Merriam-Webster's Collegiate Dictionary*

.

Loneliness

Your New Friend

"Is this seat free?

How are you this morning? What's your name? May I have the inestimable boon of a few minutes' conversation?

What brings you here? Where do you live? Are you here on business? What do you do for a crust? What is it like to be a tuna fisherman? Where did you learn to handle a boat? Can you work under pressure? How much money do you have? Can you spot me twenty-five dollars until payday? What was your name again?

What if we were rich? What is wealth without health? Do you think a man can keep body and soul together by selling coconuts? If you think you've got it bad now, how would you like to be paid to collect pebbles?

What do you want to do for the rest of your life? What's the secret of eternal happiness? How can we tell if there is a life after death? Who can tell that for a surety? How would children unpack that concept? Shall we just back-burner that one?

Are you doing anything tonight? What's your phone number? How well do you have to know someone before you call them a friend? Have you ever been to Italy? Shall we go? Can you put me up for tonight? What about going to see a film? What about a game of bridge? What about dinner at my place? May I take your smile as an indication of approval?

Why don't you stay a little? Why are you so set upon avoiding me? <u>How</u> do you mean? Could I suggest we <u>park</u> that suggestion for the moment?

Did it storm last night, or did I <u>dream</u> it? How is motor oil <u>graded</u>? How can we hope to wrest <u>sovereignty</u> away from the oligarchy and back to the people? Do all bees <u>sting</u>? Do dogs have <u>belly buttons</u>? Are humans superior to <u>animals</u>, or just different? Are humans pretty <u>mechanistic</u> beings? Why are we so interested in the private <u>affairs</u> of famous people? Is nothing sacred? (That's a <u>rhetorical</u> question, BTW.)

Are <u>you</u> listening? Are you paying <u>attention</u> to what I'm saying? What's the <u>matter</u>? Is something <u>bothering</u> you? Why are you <u>angry</u> with me? What am I doing <u>wrong</u>? Are you <u>keeping track</u> of the time? Have you checked the bus <u>timetable</u>? <u>When</u> will we leave? When will we <u>get</u> to Dallas?"

Sources: *New Oxford American Dictionary, Collins COBUILD Primary Learner's Dictionary, Collins English Dictionary, Dictionary of American Slang, Macquarie Dictionary, The American Heritage Dictionary, The American Heritage Dictionary of Idioms, NTC's Dictionary of British Slang*

Loss

Downpour

Emily underdressed, got into bed, and turned off the light. She felt burned out, an empty shell. She stared into the fog, willing it to clear.

Thomas's eyelids drowsily lifted. He felt a vestigial flicker of anger from last night. He pretended to be asleep.

It was still pouring outside. The rain enveloped them in a deafening cataract. Last year had not been, by any reckoning, a particularly good one. It had taken them the best part of ten years to move forward, to alleviate sorrow, to get her to speak.

Tears were beginning to well in her eyes. A great ocean between them, he felt for her hand. A flash of understanding or remembrance passed between them, and she began to bawl like a child.

They listened to the howl of the gale. They didn't bargain on this storm.

Sources: *New Oxford American Dictionary, Collins COBUILD Primary Learner's Dictionary, Macquarie Dictionary*

Joshua and Nicolai

It happened late in 1984. We both lived in a bubble, the kind provided by occupying a privileged pied-à-terre in Greenwich Village. Nicolai's English was much the worst, but he had the most divine smile, and short-cropped blond hair. He always had men hovering around him like bees around a honeypot. He was drinking excessive amounts of brandy, imagining himself as the last rock of civilization being swept over by a wave of barbarism. He got thrown out of bars for bellowing Portuguese folk songs.

The irony is that I thought he could help me. Young love.

He began to suffer from bouts of sleeplessness. An air of melancholy surrounded him. A night of rioting, ten detainees suffocated in an airless police cell; they took the other three away in an ambulance. Weapons were recovered from the house, including a shotgun. He began to question what had been done in his name. He was admitted to the hospital after overdosing on cocaine (I found him, trussed up in his closet).

It hurts like hell, but we learn from experience. May he rest in peace.

Source: *New Oxford American Dictionary*

Love

An Extraordinary Woman

He <u>began</u> as a drummer. She <u>studied</u> biology and botany.
He was a man of few <u>words</u>. She was <u>widely</u> read.
He was younger than <u>her</u>. She <u>longed</u> for a little more
    excitement.
He was warm and tender <u>toward</u> her. She <u>thought</u> he'd
    mistaken her for someone else.
He <u>walked</u> her home to her door. She <u>matched</u> her steps
    to his.
He <u>drew</u> a map. She bent her head to <u>study</u> the plans.

He put one hand over her shoulder and one around her waist.
    She liked the shape of his nose.
They wed a week after meeting.
She gave birth to a son. He worked like a demon.
She strove to be the perfect wife. He was a model husband
    and father.
She was forever pushing her hair out of her eyes. He waltzed
    her around the table.
The rest, as they say, is history.
He went out to the store.
She passed away peacefully in her sleep.
He reached out a hand and touched her forehead.
She was the love of his life.
He went downstairs, holding tight to the banisters.
What an extraordinary woman she was, to be sure.

Source: *New Oxford American Dictionary*

Maria

When I was seventeen, I packed my bags and left home; I had
an opportunity to go to New York and study. I left with a mix-
ture of sadness and joy—my family needed the money, so I
was obliged to work, but I felt a tug at my sleeve. It was an experience I will remember for the rest of my life.

We met during the first harsh winter after the war. The
ground was covered with ice, and the streets were full of children dressed in rags. I was alone in a strange city, a girl in a
mangy fur coat. She was a second-generation American, a
woman of supernatural beauty. She reminded me, in some in-
definable way, of my grandmother.

We went everywhere together. Her parents were both art collectors, so she was a regular visitor to the museum. She knew all the Manhattan hot spots for classy blues and retro jazz. I stood blinking in bright light. She knew what she was doing; a girl of seventeen is highly impressionable.

To a certain degree I am romancing the past, but the past is impossible to recall with any approach to accuracy. She left New York on June 6. She left a note for me. Eyes blinded with tears, I lay on the lumpy bed and listened to the noise of traffic outside as the windows rattled in the wind. I missed my mother's homemade bread.

Sources: *Collins COBUILD Primary Learner's Dictionary, New Oxford American Dictionary*

Spellcaster

I never believed in love spells or magic until I met this spellcaster. With a deft motion of his nimble fingers, he materialized a taxi out of nowhere, conjured up a most delicious homemade stew, and transformed a bare stage into an enchanted forest. We got engaged on my twenty-sixth birthday, disappeared in the twinkling of an eye, and bought a place on the lake. A magician and his glam assistant in domestic felicity.

Sources: *New Oxford American Dictionary, Collins COBUILD Primary Learner's Dictionary, The American Heritage Dictionary*

Mixology

Seasonal Craft Cocktails

The Caledonian Railway
Blended whiskey, balsamic resins, burnt orange, amber
beads, beetle.

The Metric System
Overproof rum, vin mousseux, coastal waters, dendritic salt,
medicinal herbs, nanoplankton.

Abdominal Tenderness
Crappy wine, flat champagne, a piece of rebar.

The Goldbach Conjecture
Peach schnapps, seasonal rainfall, unbruised bananas,
pasteurized milk, unpasteurized milk, larvae, spirochete,
carbuncle.

Bereavement Counseling
A quadruple vodka, fancy molasses, desiccated coconut,
generic aspirin, a pinch of snuff, a wafer of ice, a single
red rose.

Why Does Elsbeth Not Bring Forth a Child?
Three shots of well tequila, virgin snow, milkweed floss,

juniper berries, rosary beads, petrified wood, chocolate buttons, pentagram.

Chicken Supreme
Fortified wine, immature fruit, nonfat buttermilk, grass tuffets, a soupçon of mustard, antimatter.

The Landed Aristocracy
A single whiskey, peach nectar, chlorinated water, reptile eggs, striated bark, bonfire smoke, semidarkness, cherries jubilee.

The Sorrowing Widower Found It Hard to Relate to His Sons
Draft beer, instant coffee, peanut brittle, geode.

The Birthday Boy
Powerful 132-proof rum, cocoa powder, tinned fruit, popsicle sticks, Mickey Mouse ephemera.

It Will Be Interesting to Hear What the Man in the Street Has to Say about These Latest Tax Cuts. A Tax Cut for the Wealthy Will Have a Much Smaller Multiplier Effect in the Economy Than One for the Lower Economic Classes.
Straight brandy, licorice twist.

The Ethics of Euthanasia
Boric oxide, methyl bromide, cinnamon stick.

Source: *New Oxford American Dictionary*

Money

Ruth

All I <u>knew</u> was that she was a schoolteacher—a <u>temporary</u> job—and I <u>got</u> the impression that she wasn't happy.

"Sorry to <u>butt</u> in on you."

"What do you want <u>now</u>?"

"Forgive me asking an <u>indelicate</u> question, but how are you for money?"

"What do you mean? I don't <u>get</u> it."

For a <u>split second</u>, I hesitated. The studio was a <u>single</u> large room. The table was <u>strewn</u> with books and papers. Her mug was doing <u>duty</u> as a wineglass. The cat was <u>lapping</u> up a saucer of milk.

"I'm afraid I've got to <u>put</u> your rent up."

She looked <u>pale</u> and drawn. Tears were beginning to <u>well</u> in her eyes.

"I'm sorry, Ruth, I <u>really</u> am."

"I can take <u>care</u> of myself."

"It's <u>getting</u> late; I don't want to <u>take</u> up any more of your time. Sorry to <u>trouble</u> you."

She slammed the door <u>shut</u>.

"By the <u>way</u>, pay in advance if you can." I stopped and listened, <u>straining</u> my ears for any sound. Somewhere within, a harp was <u>playing</u>.

Source: *New Oxford American Dictionary*

Mountaineering

Base Camp

"Can I ask you something?"

"Yes, of course."

"Why is she here?"

"Susan and I do everything together. She's a wise woman."

"She's an eighty-three-year-old pensioner who still enjoys cycling."

"She's a bit deaf, but her mind is still sharp."

"She is now totally deaf."

"I'm sorry, I don't follow."

"You really are serious about this, aren't you?"

"She's a calm, patient woman."

"Mount Everest is the highest mountain in the world."

"As you get older, it's important to keep active."

For a few seconds, nobody spoke. A strong wind was blowing from the north.

"Well, shall we go?"

Source: *Collins COBUILD Primary Learner's Dictionary*

Murder

Noir II

The <u>midnight</u> hours. The <u>rain</u> had not stopped for days. A stranger slowly approached from the <u>shadows</u>. The walls threw back the <u>echo</u>es of his footsteps. His voice was low and shaky with <u>emotion</u>. A day's <u>growth</u> of unshaven stubble on his chin. He <u>took</u> an envelope from his inside pocket. Her <u>alabaster</u> cheeks flushed with warmth, high cheekbones <u>powdered</u> with freckles.

"We should talk somewhere less <u>public</u>."

She <u>grabbed</u> him by the shirt collar.

"We're going to settle this <u>here</u> and now." He drew a deep, <u>shuddering</u> breath. Chest <u>pains</u>. A <u>trickle</u> of blood. She was <u>smiling</u>.

"I got all <u>dolled</u> up for a party."

Source: *New Oxford American Dictionary*

Shvitz

In cocktail lounges all over town convenes the daily meeting of the ain't-it-awful <u>club</u>. Much <u>drinking</u>, little thinking. A lot of lowbrows pretending to be intellectual <u>high-hats</u>, treating the symptoms and <u>not</u> the cause.

I don't shrink from my responsibilities, but when it's time for thinking I like to have a shvitz. Sweat serves to cool down the body, to cleave a path through the wilderness, and to salve one's conscience. A whetstone for dull wits. Our great-grandfather and his brothers went to the shvitz together. They had a pleasant half hour's sit-down together, a shower, and a brisk rubdown with a towel, then they went their several ways.

In a dim room, damned hot, I sat absorbed in my own blue funk and beads of sweat. Vague forms seen through mist, two men were deep in conversation. One of them was glancing nervously around—a young man talking in broken Italian. He grumbled something about the decision being unnecessary. I plied the fire with fresh fuel and parked myself in the corner, picking up snatches of conversation:

Lost ships.

A lunatic asylum.

Reliable, accurate rifles.

A case of mistaken identity.

A geometric figure of mystical significance.

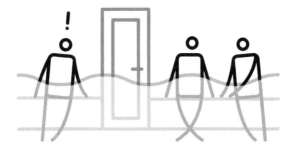

$840 million and counting.

Dumb with astonishment, I started to try to untangle the mystery, when the building's fire bell cut the conversation short and they left the room without a backward glance.

I tried the doors, but they were locked.

Sources: *New Oxford American Dictionary, Dictionary of American Slang, Macquarie Dictionary, The Home Book of Proverbs, Maxims, and Familiar Phrases*

Music

This Mixtape Is Terrible

1. A maudlin ballad.
2. A choral work.
3. A lovely little music-hall ditty.
4. Avant jazz? Electropop? Sounds like discharges of artillery.
5. A whistling noise.
6. A song for lament and sorrow.
7. A houseful of barking dogs and screaming children.
8. *The Song of Hiawatha*.
9. Inaudible pulses of high-frequency sound.
10. Taxi drivers honking their horns.
11. Mozart's symphonies in arrangements for cello and piano.
12. A wildly over-simplistic song about what it takes to be happy.
13. A chorus of boos.
14. Four-part harmony in the barbershop style (the Amazon track listing just says "Radio Edit," so who knows what you'll get).
15. A moment of silence presided over by a local minister.

16. <u>Copious</u> weeping.
17. The <u>sound</u> of the Beatles.

Sources: *New Oxford American Dictionary, Merriam-Webster's Collegiate Dictionary*

This Mixtape Is Worse

1. <u>Inarticulate</u> sounds.
2. <u>Territorial</u> growls.
3. The sound of a witch's <u>anathemas</u> in some unknown tongue.
4. Five minutes of <u>oblivion</u>, <u>deafening</u> noises, and <u>blood-curdling</u> screams.
5. <u>Dead</u> silence.
6. <u>Heavy</u> silence.
7. <u>Profound</u> silence.
8. <u>Churchlike</u> silence.
9. <u>Complete</u> silence.
10. The sound of <u>retreating</u> footsteps.

Sources: *New Oxford American Dictionary, Macquarie Dictionary, The American Heritage Dictionary, Merriam-Webster's Collegiate Dictionary*

Nature

Creatures of the Atlantic Ocean Commentary (Take 3)

Vermilion streaks of sunset on the Atlantic Ocean. The sea is thick with fish.

As teal dabble in the shallows, sailfish tail-walk along the surface of the water, in search of romance. Once their interest is aroused, they follow the scent with sleuthlike pertinacity. Large angelfish swim slowly past—they are blissfully in love. Many of the coarse fish are spawning in the vegetation. After mating, the female does not eat: the fish covers its spawn with gravel, and the eggs hatch after a week. They have the brattiest children.

Small fish are vulnerable to predators. Living in constant fear of attack. Poor little beggars.

Like gleaming seaweed that curls and undulates with the tide, fish move with the currents of the sea. At night, parrotfish are approachable as they sleep in nooks and crannies on the reef. But by day, the fish is a slippery customer and very hard to catch. They have famously reclusive lifestyles, and they go to great lengths to avoid the press. I can hardly blame them.

This fish is delicious with early potatoes and a tangy salad.

Living in the digital age can be fiercely expensive, but fish of the Atlantic coast have devious ways of making money. They enjoy playing cards, and they all play basketball, although on different teams. They don't like to trust their money to anyone outside the family, like crabs and other shelled creatures.

A six-gilled shark . . . starfish . . . cuttlefish . . . There is nothing so desperately monotonous as the sea. Can I be excused?

Sources: *New Oxford American Dictionary, Collins COBUILD Primary
Learner's Dictionary, Macquarie Dictionary, The American Heritage
Dictionary, The American Heritage Dictionary of Idioms*

Nausea

Seasick

The whiskey lit a fire in the back of his throat. He wiped his mouth with the back of his hand and lay on his back. A coded message clittered over the radio speakers. He felt his stomach clench in alarm. The distress call had given the ship's position: the fishermen were steering a direct course for Kodiak. He held on to the back of a chair. His old fears came flooding back. He was not a strong swimmer.

Source: *New Oxford American Dictionary*

Navigation

A Walk

I took the <u>alternate</u> route home, streets <u>alive</u> with traffic, <u>avenues</u> of communication, <u>abrupt</u> hills, <u>aleatoric</u> music, <u>artwork</u> being sold on the sidewalk, hotels with modern <u>amenities</u> lined up in soldierly <u>array</u>, the <u>aureate</u> light of COMING AT-TRACTIONS! AMAZINGLY LOW PRICES! AUTHENTIC MEXICAN FARE! Everything in neat <u>arrangement</u>, <u>amorous</u> couples in the bright <u>apparel</u> of spring, penniless <u>ancients</u> stood in <u>awe</u> of the king, the <u>awfully</u> rich young American in the <u>armor</u> of prosperity, <u>anthropomorphic</u> deities, movie studio <u>apparat-chiks</u>, <u>aficionados</u> of the bullfight. Civilization and its <u>attendant</u> morality. All <u>aquiver</u> with excitement, I was not moving <u>anymore</u> with my feet.

Source: *Merriam-Webster's Collegiate Dictionary*

Directions

It's quite simple, <u>chief</u>: Take the first turning on the <u>right</u>, keep <u>straight</u> on, make a <u>dogleg</u> at the fire station, and continue south. Then turn left at the <u>point</u> where you see a sign to Apple Grove. Take the first <u>right</u> over the stream, <u>bear</u> left and follow the old road, <u>hang</u> a right at the <u>semiderelict</u> farmhouse, and keep <u>straight</u> on until the road <u>peters out</u> to a rutted track. Follow the blue <u>post</u>s until the track meets a forestry road. Take a <u>left</u> here. A quarter-mile <u>walk</u> from there <u>over</u> the hill is a small village, and you can get to the beach by <u>tram</u>. <u>Charter</u> a boat, go <u>due</u> west <u>one</u> hundred miles or until the engine gives out, stay <u>there</u>, and don't come <u>back</u>.

Sources: *New Oxford American Dictionary, Collins COBUILD Primary Learner's Dictionary, Collins English Dictionary, The American Heritage Dictionary, Merriam-Webster's Collegiate Dictionary, Black's Law Dictionary*

Nitroglycerin

Detonator

As the bomb exploded five hundred yards from where he was standing, he remembered working sixteen hours straight. He remembered sitting in silence with his grandmother as evening drew on, her left eye, his skinny arms, cigarette ash and artificial flowers, his twelfth birthday, his seventeenth birthday, his father's tyrannies, his mother's nightlong laments for his father, his baby bro—his traveling companion—his quirks and quiddities: his messy hair, his maddening stories, his wizardry with leftovers. He remembered the languor and warm happiness of those golden afternoons, broad-leaved evergreens, fishing tackle and broken-spined paperbacks, a ten-pounder, his trusty Corona typewriter, a hat that he wore at a rakish angle, a gray suit flecked with white, his fruitless attempts to publish poetry, his mother's gift of a pen. He remembered the touch of her hand—his first wife—her lively mind, her delighted cackle, sleeping under canvas, the seasonal rhythm of the agricultural year, the deer season, the rainy season, the beauty and romance of the night, domestic felicity, baked apples, ambulance sirens, the hospital's east wing, the endless patience of the nurses, the abrupt finality of death. He remembered with sudden guilt the letter from his mother that he had not yet read.

Sources: *New Oxford American Dictionary*, *Collins COBUILD Primary Learner's Dictionary*, *Collins English Dictionary*

Nostalgia

I Was

I was lying prone on a foam mattress. I was having difficulty in keeping awake. I was cold and exhausted. I was tempted to look at my watch but didn't dare. I was too tired to write up my notes. I was on assignment for a German magazine. I was working like a madman. I was wallowing in the luxury of the hotel.

I was mystified, and in a fever of expectation. I was enmeshed in the surety of my impending fatherhood. I was afraid to tell anyone I was scared witless.

I was a shocker when I was younger. I was excruciatingly shy at that age. I was just a fumbling, featherheaded kid. I was going on fourteen when I went to my first gig. I was a real stoner when I was a teenager.

I was overcome with acute nostalgia for my days in college. I was a nihilistic punk with a Mohican and a ring in my nose. I was trying to decide if I should major in drama or English. I was booked, fingerprinted, and locked up for the night. I was swept along by the crowd.

I was drifting off to sleep.

I was thinking about you.

Source: *New Oxford American Dictionary*

Oo

Obsession

How Easy

Kate sat on a stool in the corner of the room. It was well after midnight, she didn't know anyone at the party except the host, and the drink had made her maudlin. It was still pouring outside. As she put up her umbrella and headed back to the car, she saw that there was a man behind her; moreover, he was staring at her.

She recognized me immediately. A startlingly good memory.

She became a widow a year ago. She doesn't usually wear much make-up, but she has beautiful bone structure and great big eyes, and she does a thirty-five-minute workout every day. She studied art in Paris, and she enjoys reading detective stories by American writers. She has few friends.

As we walked along the road in the moonlight, I felt a sudden impulse to tell her that I loved her.

The man moved closer. She found his total absence of facial expression disconcerting, and she turned quickly, rattled by his presence.

"Please just leave me alone."

She twisted her head around to look at him. He was short and bald, and he had a moustache. He was carrying a coil of rope.

She tripped and fell with a thud.

I was surprised at how easy it was. The road ahead was blocked, it was very late, and the streets were empt—

She kneed him in the groin and cracked him across the forehead. She stood for a few moments, catching her breath, turning her face upwards to the drizzling rain.

Sources: *Collins COBUILD Primary Learner's Dictionary*

Red

He stopped at the mouth of the tunnel, deep in the woods. The walls were slimy with lichens, and there was a mushroomy smell of disuse and moldering books. The cry of a strange bird sounded like a whistle or a freight train. He opened his case, took out a folder, then closed it again. He frowned as he reread the letter. He pulled up his jacket collar in the cold wind; it was plain to him what he had to do.

His daughter had disappeared thirteen years ago. Investigators suspected a thunderstorm in the area might have had something to do with the plane's disappearance. Witnesses say they saw an explosion. He put up posters around the city. Police found a corpse in a nearby river, but she was elderly and silver-haired. A scrap of red paper was found in her handbag.

He was breathing fast. He was talking to himself. He felt sick with apprehension. The light was already fading, but he pushed on, a day's growth of unshaven stubble on his chin. The walls threw back the echoes of his footsteps.

The investigation was a long and slow process. Debris from the plane was found over an area the size of a football pitch. There is a video recording of his police interview, his eyes glowing with <u>insane</u> fury. As he grew older, he seldom <u>stir</u>red from his apartment.

The end of the tunnel came into <u>view</u>: the dying embers of a fire; a pile of <u>castoff</u> clothes; a red paint <u>mark</u> on the wall. A terrible <u>realization</u> struck him. His mouth fell open as he <u>perceive</u>d the truth. The stranger gave a <u>terrible</u> smile. As he spoke, the words were accompanied by a white <u>plume</u> of breath: "It's a <u>pity</u> you arrived so late."

Sources: *New Oxford American Dictionary, Collins COBUILD Primary Learner's Dictionary*

Occult, The

Fine, If You Will Keep Asking about It, a Complete List of Everything Inside the Locked Room on the Third Floor, Which, Yes, Sometimes Leaks an Oil-like Substance and Occasionally Sounds like a Murder of Crows Molesting a Harpsichord

An <u>antique</u> clock.

A <u>stack</u> of boxes.

A <u>sacrificial</u> offering to the spirits of the <u>damned</u>, may God continue to give us his <u>blessing</u>. Now be <u>quiet</u> and go to sleep.

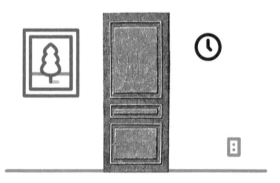

Sources: *New Oxford American Dictionary, Collins COBUILD Primary Learner's Dictionary, The American Heritage Dictionary*

Holy Smoke

The yacht made landfall under cover of darkness. Twenty or so fishing boats were moored to the pier, and the countryside was blanketed in snow. The monastery was several three-story buildings—a ruin surrounded by waist-high grass. Trembling with fear, he hauled himself along the cliff face. Smoke was billowing from the chimney. The ceremony was about to begin.

He pressed his face to the glass. There were about thirty or forty of them, grown men and women, everyone sat in a ring, holding hands. There were roses climbing up the walls, antique mirrors, hulks of abandoned machinery.

The master of ceremonies mounted the platform.

"I am Brother Joachim," he announced in a voice like thunder. His face glowed in the dull lamplight. Ardent eyes, an aquiline nose. He dug out a small hole in the snow, and a hush descended over the crowd.

"Holy smoke. Heavenly Father. Prime animator of the movement. Every soul on earth, virtuous or vicious, shall perish. Deliver us from misery, the wickedness and snares of the Devil."

He pressed a button, and the doors slid open. Now the trouble began. The machinery clunked into life and the congregation swayed, hands aloft, answering with assured and ardent yeses. Gusts of snow flurried through the door. The air smelled like a compound of diesel and gasoline fumes, and the room hummed with an expectant murmur—guttural noises, gears grinding, night sounds of birds and other creatures. For a moment the scene was illuminated, then it was plunged back into darkness.

He was thrown backward by the <u>force</u> of the explosion. As the crowd <u>panic</u>ked and stampeded for the exit, they were attacked by a swarm of <u>shadowy</u>, ethereal forms and torn <u>asunder</u>.

All at <u>once</u>, the noise stopped. The waves <u>lapp</u>ed the shore. He <u>breathe</u>d out heavily, and the air returned to the bright <u>coldness</u> of winter.

Sources: *New Oxford American Dictionary*, *Merriam-Webster's Collegiate Dictionary*

Optimism

Apology in C-sharp Minor

David took a deep <u>breath</u> and rapped on the window with his <u>knuckles</u>. Standing on the stoop of his ex-wife's house, <u>hat</u> in hand, he only had a <u>fuzzy</u> plan of action. He could dance a jig or a <u>soft-shoe</u>, but he would have to wait until his knee had <u>healed</u>.

A surge in the crowd behind him <u>jolt</u>ed him forward. The orchestra and chorus were <u>numerous</u>, and they were a very <u>disgruntled</u> crew: the woodwind <u>section</u> sat on the wall in <u>clumps</u> of two and three; the <u>first</u> violins were playing <u>pickup</u> with the <u>second</u> violins; the <u>percussion</u> section had only a <u>dim</u> notion of what was going on.

The door began to swing <u>inward</u>, the conductor <u>swept</u> her baton through the air, and the brass sections let <u>rip</u> with sheer gusto. A <u>blare</u> of trumpets, timpan<u>i</u>, the <u>lightness</u> of bow on strings. Neighbors peered <u>curiously</u> through windows.

A young man dressed in baggy pants and a <u>do-rag</u> <u>stood</u> in the doorway. The music faded in <u>discord</u>, the singers left, and the buzz <u>diminuendo</u>ed.

"Who the <u>hell</u> are you?"

Sources: *New Oxford American Dictionary, The American Heritage Dictionary, Merriam-Webster's Collegiate Dictionary*

Chin Up

As late afternoon merged imperceptibly into early evening, a warm September evening, I went for a long walk. A peaceful riverside amble before dark, where the blackwood, the box, and the bastard oak grew. Needed a change of scene.

The murmur of bees in the rhododendrons.

The birds tweeting in the branches.

Planes passing overhead.

A car horn.

A flourish of trumpet.

The scratch of a match lighting a cigarette. (I have many vices, but smoking is the big one. I blame you for that.)

There were echoes and scents that awoke some memory in me—we went for a swim in the river, but the water was a touch too chilly for us. The weather was terrible, do you remember? It was raining hard. We took a bus back to the city center, wet clothes dripping onto the floor.

Where are you living now? Are you all right? Are you keeping company with anyone special these days? Have you lost your taste for fancy restaurants?

Your problems seem larger than life at that time of night. With a suspicion of a smile, I strolled around, muttering to myself, *You'll be okay, kiddo.*

Sources: *New Oxford American Dictionary, Collins COBUILD Primary Learner's Dictionary, Collins English Dictionary, Macquarie Dictionary, Merriam-Webster's Collegiate Dictionary*

The Other Hand

I've made such a <u>mess</u> of my life. I'm all <u>washed up</u>. I lost <u>everything</u> in the crash: my friends and loved <u>ones</u>, a <u>knockout</u> wife and two daughters, a <u>flourishing</u> career . . . I didn't intend to <u>deceive</u> people into thinking it was French champagne! I never <u>dream</u>ed anyone would take offense. I was accused of <u>masterminding</u> a gold-smuggling racket, I watched my restaurant <u>burn</u> to the ground, and I was diagnosed as having a heart <u>flutter</u>. On the other <u>hand</u>, I've now reached <u>level</u> 106 on Candy Crush Saga.

Sources: *New Oxford American Dictionary*, *Collins COBUILD Primary Learner's Dictionary*, *Dictionary of American Slang*, *Macquarie Dictionary*

Order

The Life of Carlos

He was toilet-trained by the age of one.

He was bitten by the showbiz bug at the age of four.

He acted in his first professional role at the age of six.

At age seven, he was a pint-sized superstar.

He was able to read Greek at the age of eight.

He took up tennis at the age of eleven.

By his twelfth birthday, he lived a life of luxury.

At music college, the young Carlos was taught classical violin, and by the age of fourteen he was in no doubt about his career aims.

At sixteen he converted to Catholicism.

On his seventeenth birthday, he fell gravely ill.

At eighteen he was working for his dad, repping on the road.

He married at nineteen.

He was in and out of jail for most of his twenties—they divorced eight years later.

A man in his late twenties, prematurely balding, he started at the company as a machine operator.

By the time he was thirty-five, he had made a name for himself as a contractor.

A year later, he had nothing to show for his efforts.

He committed suicide at the age of forty.

Source: *New Oxford American Dictionary*

Ornithology

Robin

A bird settled on top of the hedge.

"Hello there! How are you? I was just, uh, passing by. I don't live here—I'm only visiting. I fly back to New York this evening. How's that for stamina!" He broke into song.

"I don't know about you, but I'm starving. I could murder a sandwich now."

An ibis circled low, lit on the bridge's railing, and began to preen its feathers.

"Ho ho! A stranger in our midst! Well, if it isn't Frank! How goes it?"

The bird spread its wings and soared into the air in silence. A breeze made the treetops sigh.

"Charming! What a beak on that guy. He likes to kid everyone he's the big macho tough guy." He sniffed in a deprecating way. "It's just an act."

He fluttered to the branch and perched there for a moment.

"Well, as I was saying, I feel like I've gone through the mill—I'm pooped. What people don't realize is that wings are actually very heavy. And between you and me, heights give me the horrors."

A flock of birds flew overhead.

"Elaine!" he shouted, heedless of attracting unwanted attention. "Never mind. I forget what I was going to say." There were several moments of awkward silence.

"It <u>can</u> get lonely in the evenings. The <u>birdlings</u> flew away in the autumn."

The bird flapped his <u>wings</u>.

"Do you <u>fancy</u> a drink?"

Sources: *New Oxford American Dictionary, Collins COBUILD Primary Learner's Dictionary, Collins English Dictionary, Macquarie Dictionary, NTC's Dictionary of British Slang*

Patience

The Greatest Story Never Told

"I'm going to tell you a <u>story</u>. Are you sitting <u>comfortably</u>? Here is a children's <u>fable</u> about love and honesty. It's a <u>tale</u> about the friendship between two boys, a drama about two young brothers who are <u>abrupt</u>ly abandoned by their father. It's an adventure <u>story</u>, a tragic <u>love story</u>, and an unforgettable tale of joy and <u>heartbreak</u>. You're <u>going</u> to enjoy this.

"The novel deals with several different topics: the <u>sanctity</u> of human life, the dangers of religious <u>extremism</u>, our obsession with the <u>here</u> and now, the <u>yoke</u> of marriage . . . Lots of people don't <u>bother</u> to get married these days. I <u>wonder</u> whether you have thought more about it? That's getting off the subject, but never <u>mind</u>. Nothing is more irritating than people who do not <u>keep</u> to the point. Let's get down to <u>business</u>! Shady <u>characters</u>, an <u>intriguing</u> story, a <u>touching</u> reconciliation scene . . . it's the best novel I've ever <u>read</u>. Now, let me <u>see</u>, where did I put it? <u>Ah</u>, there you are! The book was filmed as a six-part TV <u>serial</u>, and the play was adapted for the <u>big</u> screen! I didn't enjoy the film; the acting was <u>dreadful</u>, but if you like <u>steampunk</u>, this is a great book for you. Oh, look! The sun's <u>coming</u> out! I'm <u>kind</u> of thirsty. Would you <u>like</u> a cup of coffee? Shall <u>we</u> have a drink? Let's have a <u>cup</u> of coffee. <u>Hold</u> on a minute, I'll be right back.

"Are you <u>all right</u>? You were screaming. Anyway, <u>um</u>, where was I? Let me see, now; oh, yes, I remember. The book is set in the 1940s—"

Sources: *New Oxford American Dictionary, Collins COBUILD Primary Learner's Dictionary*

House White

He deliberated over the menu. Seventeen years later, he ordered a glass of Pinot Grigio.

Source: *New Oxford American Dictionary*

Speed Dates

"Hi! How are you doing? My name is John, I work in an advertising agency, I'm a good cook, I love cuddling up in front of a fire, and it's my firm belief we are the sons and daughters of Adam, thank you very much."

"Hello there, how goes it? What exactly are you looking for? I'm a simple man myself: I'm a child of the sixties and love prog rock, I'm a strict vegan, I enjoy playing darts, and I don't believe in ghosts. I really must go, that's my wife over there."

"How are you? My name is William, but friends call me Bill. At the risk of sounding slightly stalkerish: have you ever wondered what certain celebrities look like while they're sleeping?"

"M'lady! It is I! I'm interested in finding a childfree computer geek–girl with a worldview similar to mine, and I have never been one to deny the pleasures of the flesh. May I see you home? I am not above trying to bribe you."

"Where've you been all my life, beautiful? I'm fourteen years old and enjoy gaming and playing baseball. Can we go somewhere a little more private?"

"Hello there! I have four adorable Siamese cats, and I have three other cats: two moggies and one Bengal/Tonkinese cross. Do you have any pets? Have you noticed how relaxing it can feel to just sit and pet your fur child?"

"First of all, let me ask you something: Have you heard the news? This astounding piece of good fortune that has befallen me? Promise you won't tell? I know I can rely on your discretion. By the year 2000, management as we know it will not exist. We have to plan for the future. I've developed an interest in law, the geometry of spiderwebs, shrines to nature spirits, psychic powers. I know what I'm doing. I wear this crystal under my costume for luck. I have publicity photographs on my person at all times. My name is Parsons, John Parsons, Lord of the Sea. Follow me, if you please."

"How old are you? Do you live near here? Where *do* you live? What kind of car do you drive? Do you like music? Do you smoke? Do you smoke a pipe? Do you speak any foreign languages? Do you have much understanding of calculus? Which operating system do you use? Do you think green suits me? Do you think I'm too chubby? Can you keep a secret? Are you OK? You're as white as a sheet."

"Do you have any <u>change</u>? A couple of bucks'll <u>do</u> me."

Sources: *New Oxford American Dictionary*, *Collins COBUILD Primary Learner's Dictionary*, *Collins English Dictionary*, *Dictionary of American Slang*, *Macquarie Dictionary*, *The American Heritage Dictionary*, *My First Dictionary*

Table for One

Forty years, <u>there</u> or thereabouts, have elapsed. My <u>date</u> isn't going to show, it seems.

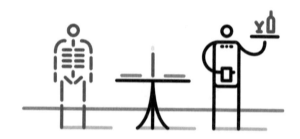

Source: *New Oxford American Dictionary*

Pity

Adrian

They were driving home when a strange <u>thing</u> happened. She saw it <u>in</u> the rearview mirror: a <u>headless</u> corpse stood <u>smack-dab</u> in the middle of the road, hands <u>unmoving</u> at his sides. She brought the car to a <u>screech</u>ing halt, and without another word turned and <u>stalk</u>ed out. Sam waited in the car, with the engine <u>run</u>ning.

"<u>What</u> do you want?"

He shrugged, feigning <u>indifference</u>. The wind <u>moane</u>d through the trees.

"Adrian," she said in her most <u>level</u> voice, "<u>spit</u> it out, man, I haven't got all day."

He thrust his hands in his pockets, <u>hunch</u>ing his shoulders. He was <u>wear</u>ing a dark suit, and his body was <u>grotesquely</u> swollen. She sighed <u>internally</u> and looked <u>into</u> the distance. She could barely see the road in the fog.

"It'<u>s</u> over. You have <u>every</u> reason to be disappointed, but you know <u>perfectly</u> well I can't stay."

He <u>gestured</u> his dissent at this.

"I can't <u>go</u> on protecting you. I'm sorry, I'm in a <u>hurry</u> and I have to go."

She <u>wrapped</u> her arms about his neck. He stood <u>stock-still</u>.

"You <u>ought</u> to wear a raincoat."

She walked away without looking <u>back</u>.

Sources: *New Oxford American Dictionary, Collins COBUILD Primary Learner's Dictionary, Collins English Dictionary, The American Heritage Dictionary*

Pizza

Rachel

Her eyes were tearful, her hands <u>trembly</u>. She felt the blood <u>drumm</u>ing in her ears, an unexpected clenching sensation in the <u>regio</u>n of her heart. Her skin was <u>deadly</u> pale. She <u>felt</u> the ground give way beneath her. Rachel shouted, beside herself with <u>fury</u>, the <u>fury</u> of a gathering storm: "GOOD PIZZA IS NOT EIGHT INCHES THICK AND <u>DROWNE</u>D IN TOMATO SAUCE."

Source: *New Oxford American Dictionary*

Prophecy

Haiku #1

A <u>sharp</u> gust of wind
The horses stopped <u>abruptly</u>—
<u>Ill</u> news travels fast.

Sources: *Collins COBUILD Primary Learner's Dictionary, Collins English Dictionary, Black's Law Dictionary*

Madame Eva

"You'll never <u>amount</u> to anything." Her voice was flat and <u>emotionless</u>.

They sat looking at each other <u>without</u> speaking. He <u>slapped</u> down a fiver. She considered him coolly <u>for</u> a moment. <u>Madame</u> Eva bent once more over the crystal ball. Her eyes <u>dilated</u> in the dark. She sat back and <u>exhaled</u> deeply.

"You'll <u>get</u> used to it."

Sources: *New Oxford American Dictionary, Collins English Dictionary*

Protest

And Another Thing

He let <u>loose</u> a stream of abuse, like water <u>gush</u>ing from a hydrant. A torrent of insults, <u>bad</u> language, and <u>bitchy</u> remarks. His <u>repertoire</u> of threats, stares, and denigratory gestures. <u>Un</u>repeatable. His breathing became <u>ragged</u>, and he began to <u>bang</u> the table with his fist. He <u>raged</u> at the futility of it all: he was <u>mouthing</u> off about society in general, <u>the</u> unemployed, the <u>republican</u> movement, his <u>first</u> wife. He stood for a few moments, catching his <u>breath</u>.

She looked <u>down</u>.

"Do you have a <u>reservation</u>?"

Sources: *New Oxford American Dictionary, The American Heritage Dictionary*

Undertow

There was a <u>mob</u> of people in the streets to see the procession. The air was <u>charged</u> with menace and noise <u>enough</u> to wake the dead.

It all happened at a tremendous <u>lick</u>.

In an <u>instantaneous</u> explosion of <u>acute</u> sorrow and <u>lawless</u> violence, panic <u>seized</u> the crowd. They all began to shout at <u>one another</u>, people of every <u>rank</u> and station filled with

141

a sudden <u>access</u> of rageful energy, and I was swept away by the <u>undertow</u>. Several policemen batoned their way into the struggling mass and <u>endeavoured</u> to restore order, though they sympathized with us in our <u>affliction</u>. They soon <u>dis-abled</u> the alarm.

I had to leave that <u>scene</u>. I was ashamed of my <u>fellow crea-tures</u>, <u>abandoni</u>ng a city to a conqueror. I wasn't <u>prepared</u> to go along with that. I <u>strolled</u> about the streets, looking in vain for a face I knew. In an alley <u>off</u> the main street, a <u>gang</u> of boys. A few yards farther on were four more, one dead and the other three so badly <u>savaged</u> I had to finish them.

The city soon <u>recovered</u> from the effects of the explosion, but when I looked in the mirror, I saw a preoccupied face, a worried head, a body out of <u>sync</u> with the mind. The man <u>that</u> I saw, there was no <u>fight</u> left in him.

Sources: *New Oxford American Dictionary*, *Macquarie Dictionary*

Qq

Quarantine

Norman

Kazuo thumped the table with his fist. There was a flash of lightning.

"I want to know what happened to Norman."

For a few seconds, nobody spoke.

"The driver lost control of his car when the tire burst. The car went off the road, knocking down a telephone pole. Mr. Forbes was sitting in the rear of the vehicle."

"What happened next?"

"He ran off, and I lost sight of him."

"Just a moment. What did you say?"

"The boy turned and ran away. In a moment, he was gone."

"How on earth did that happen? He was not even capable of standing up; he suffered injuries to his spine."

They stood motionless, staring at each other.

"We are collecting all the information relating to the crime."

"I think you've misunderstood me. Our main objective is to find the child. He is dangerously ill, and the disease is highly infectious. You must tell me everything you know."

Cal took a long, deep breath as he tried to control his emotions. He scratched his head thoughtfully and pointed the gun at the police officer.

"I really have to disagree with you there."

Source: *Collins COBUILD Primary Learner's Dictionary*

Quietude

Murmuration

"Why are you <u>angry</u> with me?"

"You're being damned <u>awkward</u>! You're trying to fit a round peg into a square hole, and it just won't <u>go</u>."

They walked on in silence for a <u>while</u>. She was red and <u>agitated</u> with the effort of arguing. He <u>swished</u> at a bramble with a piece of stick.

"I'm quite—" <u>There</u> she stopped. He placed a finger before pursed lips to <u>hush</u> her.

At this point the track entered a <u>fern gully</u>—a <u>fogbound</u> forest, air <u>heavy</u> with moisture. The breeze <u>murmured</u> in the pines, a <u>low</u> murmur, the murmuring <u>voice</u> of the forest. The

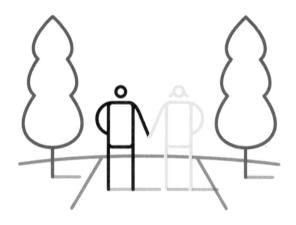

babble of a brook, the calling of a cuckoo, the expectant hush of dormant buds. Larks were warbling in the trees. Murmurous waters, soft as silk. The murmuring of the wind, the murmur of the waves, the murmur of bees in the rhododendrons. An abrupt descent from the altitudes of their anger.

She was deliberating whether or not to speak.

"It's lovely," she murmured. He nodded assent.

Sources: *New Oxford American Dictionary, Collins COBUILD Primary Learner's Dictionary, Macquarie Dictionary, The American Heritage Dictionary, Merriam-Webster's Collegiate Dictionary*

Quotation

Famous Last Words

Who the hell are you?

What's going on here?

What on earth is he doing with a spade?

Are you quite certain about this?

What is this thing for?

Where do you keep your saw?

Hold your fire until I signal.

The sea is quiet today.

Don't worry, it's cool.

Can I have the last slice of pizza?

Can I touch this wire, or is it hot?

What's that thing in the middle of the road?

At least I'm still breathing.

I'm sure there's a perfectly rational explanation.

Sorry, that witchcraft stuff is not my scene.

Get me a cocktail, my man.

Everything is going according to plan.

Come what may, I'll be home in time for dinner.

Meanwhile, folks, why not relax and enjoy the show?

Mayday. Do you copy?

Do you love me?

Do these flies bite?

I hereby declare my intention to run for public office.

I don't feel very well.

<u>Shut</u> the door.

<u>Take</u> the ax by the handle.

I would be <u>kaput</u> without a folding machete.

Where was a supersonic death ray <u>blaster</u> gun when you needed one?

If you do what I tell you, <u>then</u> there's nothing to worry about.

Yes, <u>Mr.</u> President.

Obviously this is not <u>brain surgery</u>.

This is <u>it</u>.

If I <u>should</u> die—

I guess I can <u>rest</u> awhile, with you here to watch over me.

Sources: *New Oxford American Dictionary*, *Collins COBUILD Primary Learner's Dictionary*, *Collins English Dictionary*, *Dictionary of American Slang*, *Macquarie Dictionary*, *The American Heritage Dictionary*, *The American Heritage Dictionary of Idioms*, *NTC'S Dictionary of British Slang*, *Merriam-Webster's Collegiate Dictionary*, *Black's Law Dictionary*

Recall

Poor John

We <u>met</u> at an office party. He asked me for a <u>light</u>. The <u>flare</u> of the match lit up his face, and his impassive, fierce stare <u>re-minde</u>d me of an owl. He seemed to <u>tower</u> over everyone else. A man of refreshing <u>candor</u>, with the easy <u>gait</u> of an athlete. Good <u>diction</u>. We <u>sneake</u>d out by the back exit.

The smell of a black-currant bush has ever since <u>recalled</u> to me that evening. Bonfire <u>smoke</u>. <u>Firework</u> displays. The plays <u>of</u> Shakespeare. The paintings <u>of</u> Rembrandt. <u>Greasy</u> food. <u>Experimental</u> music. <u>Rich</u>, hoppy beers. Poor John always en-joyed a drink. <u>Anyway</u>, he died last year. To make a long <u>story</u> short, I married Stephen.

Sources: *New Oxford American Dictionary, Macquarie Dictionary*

The Ten Commandments, from Memory

1. Thou shalt have <u>none</u> other gods before me.
2. Thou shalt love thy neighbor as <u>thyself</u>.
3. You <u>shall</u> not steal.
4. . . . <u>patience</u> is a virtue?
5. Don't talk to <u>strangers</u>.
6. Don't make money your <u>god</u>.
7. <u>Do</u> your best.

8. Don't put the potato skins down the <u>garbage disposal</u>.
9. Always give cyclists plenty of <u>clearance</u>.
10. God <u>save</u> the queen.

Sources: *New Oxford American Dictionary, Macquarie Dictionary, The Home Book of Proverbs, Maxims and Familiar Phrases*

Recruitment

West Adams, 11 p.m.

We met by <u>accident</u> at a party in Los Angeles. The music was so loud that I had to <u>strain</u> to hear what she was saying. She was a tall, dark <u>woman</u> with an unusual face—a <u>work</u> of art. She wore <u>pink</u> lipstick. She wore a <u>cream</u> silk shirt and a blue skirt with white <u>stripes</u>. I was sure <u>I'd</u> seen her before.

We went down some <u>steps</u> into the garden, and she put some dry <u>sticks</u> on the fire. There was something <u>strange</u> about the way she spoke. She told me her husband was <u>dead</u>, that she was from a traditional <u>Jewish</u> family. She <u>gazed</u> into the fire. The color suddenly <u>faded</u> from her cheeks.

"Have you ever <u>fired</u> a gun before?"

I stared at her <u>blankly</u>.

"How happy are you with <u>regard</u> to your work?"

Her bracelets <u>jingled</u> on her thin wrist. We looked at <u>each</u> other in silence. She gave a little <u>smile</u>.

"You really are <u>serious</u> about this, aren't you?"

She threw a <u>bucket</u> of water on the fire.

"You can <u>reach</u> me at this phone number."

Source: *Collins COBUILD Primary Learner's Dictionary*

Reenactment

He Said

When I met Jill, I was living on my own. We were in full dress, with fore-and-aft hats and swords, standing waist-deep in the river.

(The re-enactment of a naval battle on the village green.)

It was three o'clock before the king's army was embattled. The enemy circled the hill, black ravens emerged from the fog, and I braced myself for the inevitable blast. At that moment, there was a sound of a car honking plaintively—she dunked herself down to the neck with a gasp of shock at the coldness and an involuntary laugh. Everyone thought she was a riot. I watched her in awed silence.

It was a good, clean fight. We fought shoulder to shoulder with the rest of the country, she died in battle, then we went for a drink.

What attracted me to her was her animality, her adamantine will. We got engaged on my twenty-sixth birthday, bought a condo in a new development built by the river. We'd sit and talk about jazz, make dinner, make merry.

The marriage lasted for less than two years. There's no need to go into it now.

I pictured her again as she used to be: a steady, lambent light, a valiant warrior with flags aflutter. An echo of the past in the pale, chill light of an October afternoon.

Sources: *New Oxford American Dictionary, Collins COBUILD Primary Learner's Dictionary, Collins English Dictionary, Macquarie Dictionary, The American Heritage Dictionary*

She Said

I was on the <u>rebound</u> when I met Jack. We were in full dress, with <u>fore-and-aft</u> hats and swords, standing waist-<u>deep</u> in the river.

(I only went along for a <u>lark</u>—a <u>personal</u> favor to a <u>mutual</u> friend.)

I was shaking from <u>head</u> to toe, my feet were <u>numb</u> with cold, and, even more <u>annoyingly</u>, I couldn't find my phone. The <u>horrors</u> of war! But he gave me an encouraging smile, and everything was <u>jake</u> again.

He had an Irish <u>accent</u>, he was short and <u>square</u>, and he seemed old before his <u>time</u>. <u>Oddly</u> enough, I liked him. We put <u>up</u> a brave fight, he died in <u>battle</u>, then we went to a wine bar and got totally <u>hammered</u>. We got along <u>famously</u>.

We were married in the <u>middle</u> of December. Pretty ridiculous, I know, but <u>there</u> it is. I don't have anything <u>insightful</u> to say about that; I was <u>nuts</u> about him. We often finished each other's sentences—we were on the same <u>wavelength</u>. He accepted me without question, in all my <u>imperfection</u>.

Took the divorce <u>hard</u>. There's no need to <u>go</u> into it now.

I <u>black</u>ed out many of my wartime experiences, but as years go <u>by</u> I remember that <u>distant</u> afternoon, soldiers standing <u>sentinel</u> with their muskets.

Sources: *New Oxford American Dictionary*, *Collins COBUILD Primary Learner's Dictionary*, *Macquarie Dictionary*, *The American Heritage Dictionary*

Relationships

Fifty More Ways to Leave Your Lover

A fire escape.
A getaway car.
A luxury yacht.
A formal complaint.
An uncomfortable silence.
The 100-meters sprint.
A trick question.
A divine revelation.
A foregone conclusion.
A humiliating defeat.
A tearful farewell.

A leaked government document.

A blunt statement of fact.

A bleak prophecy of war and ruin.

A fabulous two-week vacation.

A lack of common decency and sensitivity.

A deliciously inventive panoply of insults.

A joke in very bad taste, the one about the chicken farmer and
the spaceship.

Clutching a large black Bible under your arm.

Stowed away on a ship bound for South Africa.

In the labyrinths beneath central Moscow.

Undercooked meats.

A hallucinatory fantasy.

Struggling under mountainous debts.

Nitpicking over tiny details.

Chasing after something you can't have.

A dozen bottles of sherry.

A fifth of whiskey on a very hot evening in July.

Alcohol dependence.

Screaming incomprehensible blasphemies at one o'clock in
the morning.

Sheer wanton vandalism.

Holding a corrections officer at knifepoint.

A misunderstanding of the facts and the law.

Compulsory military service.

Accusations of bribery.

Incontrovertible proof.

Under the guise of friendship.

A mood of resigned acceptance.

A series of lies and deceits.

A feeling of inferiority.

An aching feeling of nostalgia.

A serendipitous encounter.

A beautiful young woman.

An attractive, charismatic man.

A careless error.

A narrow escape.

A short speech.

A natural death.

A pretentious literary device.

Murder most foul.

Sources: *New Oxford American Dictionary, Macquarie Dictionary*

Religion

Grace

Before dinner, the Reverend Newman said <u>grace</u>: "<u>Heavenly</u> Father. What kind of a <u>heel</u> do you think I am? How <u>dare</u> you talk to me like that! Don't <u>give</u> me any of your back talk, smart-<u>ass</u>. It's been an absolute <u>bastard</u> of a week. I <u>sin</u>ned and brought shame down on us. As <u>far</u> as I'm concerned, it's no big deal. I suppose you believe that <u>rubbish</u> about vampires. The allegations were <u>false</u>, do you understand <u>me</u>? Why don't you leave me alone? Go on, get <u>lost</u>! I'll <u>get</u> mine, you get yours, we'll all get wealthy. <u>Amen</u> to that!"

Source: *New Oxford American Dictionary*

Savagery

Crime Scene

A <u>peremptory</u> knock on the door. <u>Unearthly</u> quiet. Hank, already sweltering, began to sweat <u>still</u> more profusely. He kicked the door open, <u>drew</u> his gun, and peered into the gloomy apartment. It was too dark to <u>distinguish</u> anything more than their vague shapes. He felt a <u>grip</u> at his throat. He <u>point</u>ed the flashlight beam at the floor. The room was a <u>shambles</u>—their throats had been cut and they lay in a waste of blood, piles of dirty <u>laundry</u>.

He closed his eyes and <u>sagged</u> against the wall.

"Damn it to <u>hell</u>."

The <u>creak</u> of a floorboard broke the silence. The flashlight <u>beam</u> dimmed perceptibly, and he came <u>face-to-face</u> with a tiger.

"You're late," he <u>growl</u>ed.

Sources: *New Oxford American Dictionary*, *Collins English Dictionary*

Root and Branch

They arrived <u>all</u> together <u>in</u> darkness, an <u>unstoppable</u> army in <u>astronomical</u> number. They destroyed us root and branch, columns of men five <u>abreast</u> with reliable, <u>accurate</u> rifles. We were <u>hunt</u>ed from our ground, shot, poisoned, and had our daughters, sisters, and wives taken from us.

Thrown into chaos, breathless from running, we attempted to swim the swollen river. We unfastened a boat from its moorings and hung on like grim death as the current drifted the boat to sea, and the thunder of the surf became a muted whisper. Looking back at the pewter sky, faces ashen and haggard, we said nothing.

Now there are just twelve of us in all. Some of us have a lower resistance to cold than others.

Where are we going? What exactly are we looking for? Where do we live? We have no ready-made answers. How do butterflies navigate when they migrate? Birds winging the air, wind bellying the sails, I persist in dangling over the boat side to dabble in the clear, deep, running water.

Sources: *New Oxford American Dictionary*, *Macquarie Dictionary*, *The American Heritage Dictionary*, *Merriam-Webster's Collegiate Dictionary*

Sea, The

Captain

The engines stopped, and the craft <u>coast</u>ed along. Gulls and cormorants bobbed on the <u>wave</u>s. A <u>reverent</u> silence. A memorial to the <u>lost</u> crewmen.

Normally the boat is <u>crew</u>ed by five people. Team members are more effective than individuals working <u>alone</u>. I had to do it, I had no <u>choice</u>.

Source: *New Oxford American Dictionary*

Self-Doubt

Fair Dismissal

Maybe they thought I was a sexual deviant, some rock spider lurking in wait. Maybe the singularity just happened, and I didn't notice. Maybe I dreamed it. Maybe I'm too close to the forest to see the trees, if you catch my drift. Maybe I acted too hastily. Maybe the world isn't on my case—maybe the problem is me. Maybe I picked the wrong career after all.

Sources: *New Oxford American Dictionary, Dictionary of American Slang*

Reviews Are In

"Five hundred contiguous dictionary entries? Who wrote this puke?"

"This book would deprave and corrupt young children."

"A profoundly disturbing experience."

"The book is rather colorless, like its author. Jumps from one subject to another. Awkward writing, hollow characters, and leaden dialogue. Personally, I think it's overrated."

"The work of a bungling amateur. He writes in broad, inaccurate <u>brushstrokes</u> and seems incapable of grasping the meaning of his own words."

"In the most abominable passage of his <u>ghastly</u> little book, he writes repetitive and <u>uninspired</u> poetry."

"A titanic <u>tower</u> of garbage."

"For readers seeking illumination, this book <u>might</u> as well have been written in Serbo-Croatian."

"Convicted <u>murderers</u>, I <u>guarantee</u> that you'll like this book."

Sources: *New Oxford American Dictionary*, *Collins English Dictionary*, *Dictionary of American Slang*, *The American Heritage Dictionary*

Self-Help

How to Win Friends and Influence People

A <u>firm</u> hand

A <u>commanding</u> presence

A basket of <u>homegrown</u> fruit and <u>individually</u> wrapped
cheeses

<u>Sedulous</u> flattery

<u>Scintillating</u> conversation

<u>Oral</u> hygiene

<u>Black</u> magic

A portrait in <u>oils</u>

A display of traditional <u>Slovakian</u> folk dancing

A <u>sweet</u> sports car

Half a <u>billion</u> dollars

Dirty, <u>lowdown</u> tricks

A crucial <u>piece</u> of evidence

A death <u>hex</u>

A little <u>diddy</u> baby hedgehog

Sources: *New Oxford American Dictionary*, *Macquarie Dictionary*,
Merriam-Webster's Collegiate Dictionary

Siblings

Visiting Hours

They stood in <u>silence</u>, <u>sheltere</u>d from the rain under a tree. He looked up at the clock in the church <u>tower</u>. It was ten o'clock.

"The hospital <u>staff</u> were very good."

She nodded <u>sympathetic</u>ally.

Ray and his sister lived just twenty-five miles <u>apart</u>, but they spoke very <u>little</u>. He had nothing in <u>common</u> with his sister. Oil and water don't <u>mix</u>.

"Don't <u>worry</u>, I'm sure he'll be fine."

A <u>flock</u> of birds flew overhead. She looked at him in <u>disbe-lief</u>.

"I don't think you fully <u>comprehend</u> what's happening. This is only a <u>short-term</u> solution."

They stood <u>motionless</u>, staring at each other. She leaned <u>against</u> him. <u>Suddenly</u>, she looked ten years older.

Source: *Collins COBUILD Primary Learner's Dictionary*

Sports

Pep Talk

"<u>Listen</u> up, everybody. I saw a <u>lotta</u> courage out there, and a lotta hard work, but we need to be <u>permanently</u> vigilant. It's time to get over the <u>butthurt</u> from last year's playoffs. No more <u>chickenshit</u> excuses. Let's skip the <u>guilt trip</u> and talk real, rational reasons. We have to plan <u>ahead</u>. Don't let them <u>stampede</u> us into anything. It's a <u>jungle</u> out there, and I need people prepared to go out and <u>graft</u>. We have the team that can win the championship, <u>providing</u> we avoid bad injuries, but we will have to <u>pay the piper</u>, and the price is apt to be a high one.

"Now, I can't remember every <u>little</u> detail, but <u>very</u> quickly, I am going <u>to</u> tell you a story. There once <u>was</u> a man. A brilliant man, <u>great</u> at mathematics, a real <u>Joe College</u> type. He was born deaf and without the power of <u>speech</u>, but he worked like a demon; he made millions upon millions <u>sniffing</u> out tax loopholes for companies, then he died after falling down a <u>lift shaft</u>. The <u>moral</u> of this story is that one must see the beauty in what one has. <u>Pardon</u> me, the <u>moral</u> of this story is that no good ever came of a man winning the lottery. The <u>lottery</u> of . . . life. <u>Hold</u> on, wait a <u>minute</u>. No, the <u>moral</u> of this sad story is 'Do not trust anyone,' or make sure that you set goals that are <u>reachable</u> but don't <u>undersell</u> yourself. Nobody can predict the <u>future</u>. Basic<u>ally</u>, don't waste time <u>looking</u> back on things that have caused you distress, remember to drink <u>responsibly</u>, and don't buy a hard bed in the <u>mistaken</u> belief that it is good for—Wait, don't go <u>yet</u>!"

Sources: *New Oxford American Dictionary, Collins COBUILD Primary Learner's Dictionary, Macquarie Dictionary*

A Short British Argument

"How can I put this politely? Will you be so kind as to <u>fuck off</u>?"

"Look, you <u>jumped-up</u> little nothing, watch your tongue."

"Why don't you do the smart thing and clear off, <u>John</u>?"

"Why don't you go and <u>take a running jump</u> at yourself, you creep."

"Look, just <u>piss off</u>, all right? <u>Sling yer hook</u>!"

"<u>Drop dead</u>! Get lost!"

"<u>Sod off</u>! How often do you have to be told?"

"<u>Go and take a flying leap at yourself</u>! Get out of my life!"

"Just get out of my sight, you <u>pillock</u>."

"Why must you <u>cock everything up</u>?"

"How can you be such a <u>prannet</u>?"

"Do I have to <u>twist your arm</u>, or will you cooperate?"

"You're <u>pathetic</u>."

"*You're* <u>pathetic</u>."

"<u>Sod this for a game of soldiers</u>. I'm off."

"Oh, stop <u>bleating</u>, will you? I'm sorry. Let's stop arguing and <u>bury the hatchet</u>."

"<u>All kidding aside</u>, I hate to lose at croquet."

Sources: *NTC's Dictionary of British Slang, The American Heritage Dictionary of Idioms*

Tt

Technology

Keynote

"Over the centuries, <u>man</u> has asked himself many profound questions: What are we all doing <u>here</u>? <u>Where</u> are we going? What can we expect for the future of <u>mobile communication</u>?

"The <u>solution</u> to these mysteries? A thing <u>hardly</u> bigger than a credit card. It's not a computer, nor <u>anything</u> like a computer—it's a whole new branch of chemistry, a new science, if you <u>like</u>. A whole new <u>ball game</u>. The product is the <u>culmination</u> of thirteen years of research, half a <u>billion</u> dollars, and an <u>expedition</u> to the jungles of the Orinoco. It is necessary, <u>indeed</u> indispensable.

"It's a <u>slimline</u> phone, a camera with a <u>built-in</u> zoom lens, a <u>pneumatic</u> drill, a <u>bar</u> of soap, and a powerful industrial <u>combine</u>. With a <u>push</u> of a button it leaves hair feeling soft and <u>manageable</u>, and it brews a perfect blend of coffee <u>every</u> time. It <u>bench-tests</u> two times faster than the previous version and it can be molded and shaped at <u>will</u>, though it must be stored <u>either</u> in the fridge or in a cool place.

"It's a marvelous design, because it's comfortable, it's <u>practical</u>, and it actually looks good. It does what it says it does, with no design <u>gimmickry</u>. <u>How</u> does it work? <u>Beats</u> me."

Sources: *New Oxford American Dictionary*, *Collins English Dictionary*, *The American Heritage Dictionary*, *Merriam-Webster's Collegiate Dictionary*

Tedium

Your Dream

"I just had the most awful dream! I was in the gym, lifting weights, when—"

    Tina ran off wailing.

Sources: *New Oxford American Dictionary*, *Collins COBUILD Primary Learner's Dictionary*

Television

News at Eleven

Here is a short <u>summary</u> of the news: The years <u>steal</u> by, <u>fleet</u> of foot. We act as though we have <u>godlike</u> powers to decide our own destiny, but we forget that just above our heads hangs the <u>Damoclean sword</u> of our own design. <u>Faced</u> with a problem, we lie watching the clouds <u>scud</u>ding across the sky, we <u>guzzle</u> our beer and devour our pizza, we stick with our own <u>kind</u>. We stand again at a historic <u>crossroads</u>: A time of political <u>uncertainty</u> and <u>apocalyptic</u> imagery, <u>racial</u> hatred, and the wanton <u>destruction</u> of human life. <u>Gross</u> negligence, mass <u>extinctions</u>, <u>tropical</u> diseases, <u>conflict</u>s between church and state. The collapse of civilization and the return to <u>barbarism</u>. We should not <u>meekly</u> accept this fate. I know things are hard, but we have to <u>battle</u> through, from the vague regions of <u>celestial</u> space to stony <u>ground</u>. We must be <u>committed</u> to peace. We must be <u>eternally</u> vigilant. We must <u>grasp</u> the opportunities offered. That <u>goes</u> for all of us. We will return after these <u>messages</u>.

Sources: *New Oxford American Dictionary, Macquarie Dictionary, Collins COBUILD Primary Learner's Dictionary*

Theater, The

Hamlet: A Book Report

Hamlet is the classic example of a tragedy. The book is a historical thriller. Beginning at Act 1, Scene 1—a car chase—the story goes that he had gone to the board of directors with his new robot design and cut a deal, he saw the ghost of a dead man, he tried to poison his wife, and now he's mixed up in a $10 million insurance swindle. I can't remember every little detail, but Act 2 has a really funny scene—the famous underwater sequence. He's fallen out with his friends and he believes that an evil spirit has put a curse on his business, so Hamlet turns to face upstage and he makes a wish: "Heavenly

172

Father, that's <u>enough</u>, pack it in." I don't remember the <u>exact</u> words. The play is hilariously <u>funny</u>. I <u>gave</u> it five out of ten.

Sources: *New Oxford American Dictionary, Collins COBUILD Primary Learner's Dictionary*

Intermission

I seized Nathan and <u>hurl</u>ed him into the lobby.

"<u>Do</u> you like it? Isn't it <u>something</u>? Just a <u>minute</u>—where do you think you're going?"

"It's <u>late</u>, I have to get back."

"This is intense, moving, and inspiring <u>theater</u>!"

"One of the actresses <u>pretend</u>ed to urinate into a bucket."

"'Judge not the <u>play</u> before the play be done'!"

"See you <u>Wednesday</u>."

Sources: *New Oxford American Dictionary, Collins English Dictionary, The Home Book of Proverbs, Maxims and Familiar Phrases*

Timing

Maggie

"We need to talk, Maggie."

Her brow wrinkled.

"I haven't been totally honest with you."

Her mind went blank.

"It's about time I came clean and admitted it."

Her eyes moistened.

He began to apologize with copious tears and self-abasement, when, equipped with cameras and LED lights, a flash mob of 135 people appeared out of nowhere to put on a performance.

Source: *New Oxford American Dictionary*

The Usual Suspect

"Good morning, madam. First of all, I'd like to thank you for coming. Let me take your coat. Blue suits you, sets off the color of your hair. Please sit down. Would you like a cup of tea? I would imagine they'll be here soon. Please fill in this form and sign it at the bottom. You have beautiful eyes. What's that? You can fill in the missing details later. You're looking very fit; I can tell you exercise regularly. Are you doing anything tonight? I'm ever so sorry, I don't know what's come over me.

I don't suppose you could ever <u>care</u> for me seriously. Do you <u>have</u> any brothers or sisters? I'm just <u>kid</u>ding.

"<u>Well</u>, what do you think? One of these men is the <u>murderer</u>."

Sources: *New Oxford American Dictionary*, *Collins COBUILD Primary Learner's Dictionary*, *Collins English Dictionary*

Uu

Ultimatums

Either/Or

Sink <u>or</u> swim

Coffee <u>or</u> tea

<u>Hush</u> money or a river<u>bed</u>

A <u>truthful</u> answer or a <u>plausible</u> excuse

A <u>deep</u> breath or a <u>torrent</u> of abuse

A <u>dim</u> figure in the dark kitchen or just a <u>figment</u> of the imagination

<u>Afraid</u> of ghosts or <u>afraid</u> to die

<u>Intense</u> anxiety or a <u>cardiac</u> arrest

<u>Times</u> have changed or <u>you've</u> changed

<u>Halcyon</u> years or a <u>short</u> memory

Local <u>beliefs</u> and customs or <u>juju</u> and witchcraft

A simple life of prayer and personal <u>austerity</u> or acid <u>trips</u>, <u>illicit</u> sex, <u>fabulous</u> riches, and <u>gratuitous</u> violence

Fear of <u>eternal</u> damnation or a shrug of <u>resignation</u>

Sources: *New Oxford American Dictionary*, *Collins English Dictionary*, *Macquarie Dictionary*, *The American Heritage Dictionary*, *Merriam-Webster's Collegiate Dictionary*

Unhappiness

Haiku #2

Hacked down the saplings
Inarticulate with rage—
Enough already.

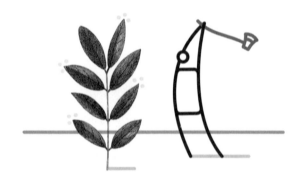

Sources: *The American Heritage Dictionary*, *Macquarie Dictionary*, *Merriam-Webster's Collegiate Dictionary*

Unknown, The

Manhole

The night was <u>percolating</u> with an expectant energy. Thousands of people <u>pack</u>ed into the city's main square, police vans were <u>park</u>ed on every street corner, and a solid <u>phalanx</u> of reporters and photographers stood <u>poised</u> for the jump.

He lifted the manhole cover and peered into the <u>depths</u> beneath.

Who <u>ever</u> heard of a grown man being frightened of the dark?

He broke out in a <u>profuse</u> sweat, <u>took</u> a deep breath, and <u>climb</u>ed down the ladder.

The silence was broken by an <u>almighty</u> roar, <u>territorial</u> growls, and the sound of a sort of <u>confused</u> hammering and shouting. The light began to <u>fail</u> and a series of deafening <u>detonation</u>s was heard, a cracking sound like a <u>rifle shot</u>. My stomach <u>heaved</u>.

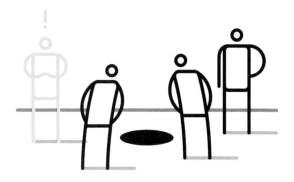

It was several minutes before he emerged, ashen-faced. He was warmly applauded, and his hand was pumped by well-wishers and gushing television commentators. All the bells of the city began to peal. Furiously, he elbowed his way through the crowd. He looked different somehow, a counterfeit image of reality. The crowd cheered and then grew still.

Tense with expectancy, I waited for my name to be called.

Sources: *New Oxford American Dictionary*, *Collins English Dictionary*, *The American Heritage Dictionary*

Onward, Seaward

One afternoon, in the throes of my unspoken passion, I walked far into the bush to remove a weight from my mind. I walked out from between thin saplings of second-growth forest to find everything out of trim. The storm had washed seaweed high on the beach. Bark shingles, scattered fragments of rock, the top hamper of some large ship.

I stood there gawping. The broad expanse of ocean, clouds sailing overhead, deadly pale, deadly dull. I was there by accident.

"Onward. Seaward."

I seemed to hear someone calling. The gentle breeze wafted the sound of voices.

"The storm approaches. Step forward. Onward, seaward."

A company of mynahs chattered on a nearby tree.

"You cannot go by what is written. Fall into the water. Start afresh. Onward, seaward."

From the bottom of my heart, the action of wind upon a ship's sails.

In keeping with my character, I leapt in <u>feet</u> first, the amen to a life which, like most lives, had once been <u>flush</u> with promise. Two short <u>steps</u> into this place, and where will they end? Who will I meet in there, and where will the meeting lead? On<u>ward</u>, sea<u>ward</u>.

Source: *Macquarie Dictionary*

Vv

Vendettas

Going to Istanbul

As the train thundered through the night, an icy breeze filtered through the open window, chilling the compartment. The aurora metropolis filled the whole of the southern horizon like an unattended fire, embers glowing in the darkness. 3:15 showed on the clock, and Lisa lay sleepless.

She stared, slit-eyed, down the length of the gun, gripping the handle until her knuckles whitened. Eyes shining with expectation, she pictured Benjamin waiting. His backswept hair, his oily smile. His last agony, in the dusk of an Istanbul nightclub. Like a cat stalking a bird, she need only wait. Put him in a box and put the box in a hole, then the matter is closed.

A voice stirred her from her reverie—a cry that sank down into an inarticulate whine. She jumped up, swung full around. There was a dull thud as her gun discharged, an uncomprehending silence, and a faint gurgling noise. She felt the ground give way beneath her.

The train jerked forward. She knelt and bowed her head by the still body of the young woman. She sat gnawing her underlip. Eyes ashine in the darkness, she sat immobile for a long time in the tranquil clacketing of the train, until it was time to go.

Sources: *New Oxford American Dictionary, The American Heritage Dictionary, NTC's Dictionary of British Slang, Merriam-Webster's Collegiate Dictionary*

Vice

Attention, Passengers

We would <u>like</u> to apologize for the late running of this service. Some crazy <u>shit</u> happened last night. Pete and Gary went out and got <u>annihilated</u>. Freddy got hold of some bad <u>acid</u> and freaked out. The party had <u>hardly</u> started when the police arrived. I was booked, <u>fingerprinted</u>, and locked up for the night. Anyway, <u>um</u>, where was I? The train is <u>due</u> to arrive at 11:15. <u>Quit</u> moaning. Don't expect anything and you won't be disappointed, that's my <u>philosophy</u>. Please have your tickets ready for <u>inspection</u>. I'm gonna <u>throw up</u>.

Sources: *New Oxford American Dictionary*, *NTC's Dictionary of British Slang*

Virginity

Whatever Floats Your Boat

I want my defloration to be a slow and sensual, transcendent rite of passage. And I don't mean just mask and flippers, boots and cap—anyone can do that! I mean oxygen cylinders, spear gun, monocle, cork-tipped cigarette—the whole dang shooting match. The sexual business is just the icing on the cake.

Source: *Macquarie Dictionary*

Wanderlust

Vanishing Point

He pressed a button, and the doors slid open. Her eyes glittered with excitement. The year was 1840, and the streets were full of children dressed in rags. Long rows of grim, dark housing developments, and the cozy fug of the music halls. His brow wrinkled.

He went over to the door and gave it a kick. A light flashed on the console, and the years rolled by: The Mesozoic era. The Edwardian era. The dawn of civilization. The Monday before last. A sudden bright flash, and the engine sputtered and stopped. They looked at each other in silence.

"I think I can smell something burning."

He stuck his head out of the door. A vast untenanted land stretched to the north of them, a coastline indented by many fjords. He walked out before she could frame a reply, and started dicking around with the controls. He was about to shut off the power when he heard her indrawn breath, and the door shut behind him. He watched the time machine dematerialize.

A flicker of amusement passed over his face. A bitter wind blew from the north. With a mood of resigned acceptance, he sat down at the base of a tree, as the sea below laved the shore with small, agitated waves.

Sources: *New Oxford American Dictionary, Collins COBUILD Primary Learner's Dictionary, Collins English Dictionary*

Weather

Rains

I was about to leave when it began to rain. A hard rain. A shroud of rain. The rain beat against the windowpanes, the rain beat down on the roof. The rain enveloped us in a deafening cataract.

Basically, it was pissing down.

I was standing in the porch because it was raining—my leather jacket is useless in the rain. It rained heavily all day, and the rain continued all night. The next day it was still bucketing down, low clouds and squalls of driving rain. Many wore rain boots and jackets, angling their umbrellas to fight the wind and rain, splashing through deep puddles. Rainwater guttered the hillside, rain poured down, pitting the bare earth, rain banked the soil up behind the gate, watered the garden. Rain beat the trees, trees that sheltered the cows. A shelter for hikers, too: the rain permeated her anorak, rain dripped from the brim of his old hat. (You have to be in the right frame of mind to enjoy hiking in the rain.) Rain made conditions all the worse. Rain stopped play. The game was abandoned because of rain—heavy rain turned the pitch into a mud bath. The rain put the kibosh on our beach party. The rain poured down, day after day. Two weeks of nonstop rain. Six inches of rain fell in a twenty-four-hour period. More than thirty inches of rain fell in six days.

At one o'clock, the rain ceased. I went for a long walk. The sky was half-blue, half-fleeced with white clouds. The soil was saturated. A mist rose out of the river. It was cold, and there was a continuous sighing in the treetops. The storm grumbled in the distance. There was a rainbird somewhere quite near, singing its sort of sad song even though it didn't even look like rain.

Sources: *New Oxford American Dictionary, Collins COBUILD Primary Learner's Dictionary, Collins English Dictionary, Macquarie Dictionary, The American Heritage Dictionary, The American Heritage Dictionary of Idioms*

Widowhood

Something to Be Glad About

She had lived alone <u>ever</u> since her husband died, and with the <u>passing</u> of the years she had become a little eccentric—a town perched on <u>top</u> of a hill, a town full of <u>color</u> and character, <u>labyrinthine</u> streets and alleys, <u>smiling</u> groves and terraces, the mountains towering all <u>around</u>, the setting sun throwing the snow-covered peaks into <u>relief</u>, the spires and <u>clustered</u> roofs of the old town wise <u>beyond</u> all others, the <u>bricks-and-mortar</u> banks, the palazzo built <u>around</u> a courtyard, the bridge <u>across</u> the river, the cobbled streets <u>running</u> down to the tiny harbor, beside the boathouse a jetty <u>thrusting</u> out into the water, the <u>roar</u> of the sea, the ringing <u>of</u> bells, the moon's pale light casting <u>soft</u> shadows.

She made a <u>point</u> of taking a walk each day, through that town perched on <u>top</u> of a hill. This was her métier, doing things; she had no attacks of self-doubt, no <u>second thoughts</u> now that her mind was made up. She was alive, which was something to be <u>glad</u> about.

Sources: *New Oxford American Dictionary, Macquarie Dictionary*

Wine

Tasting Notes

A red wine full of ripe, plummy fruit, this Cabernet has a dense, tightly woven mouthfeel, with complex, chewy, and velvety tannins and an interesting medley of flavors: caramel ice cream, burnt orange, traces of acid, and the murky silt of a muddy pond.

A smooth Bordeaux that is gutsy enough to accompany steak, this wine consistently came out top in our tastings. A heady, exotic perfume of juniper berries, marmalade, and throat lozenges. Like an emotionally dysfunctional businessman, or a land-locked sailor.

A wine with a zingy, peachy palate and a tone of condescension.

A gloriously rich Cabernet-dominated wine with clean, fresh, natural flavors. Excitement, mischief, the fresh note of bergamot, and the collected works of Edgar Allan Poe.

A full-bodied red wine with real class. Rich, ripe flavors emanate from this wine like a waft of bells, or the gentle parp of a military band, or the faint murmur of voices playing dice for high stakes as the last piece of the sun is eclipsed by the moon and the first peals of thunder roll across the sky.

A <u>young</u> wine. I can smell <u>sour</u> milk and homemade chicken <u>soup</u>.

Sources: *New Oxford American Dictionary, Collins COBUILD Primary Learner's Dictionary, Macquarie Dictionary, Collins English Dictionary, Merriam-Webster's Collegiate Dictionary*

Writing

Researching *Lycaon pictus*, or The African Wild Dog

The dust settled. The sun was high in the sky. Savaged by a wild dog, not a drop to drink, he lay on his back. Things hadn't gone entirely according to plan. The horses had galloped away, his cheek was tattooed with a winged fist, his eyes were open but he could see nothing. He had an ambitious, albeit unformed, idea for a novel. Would that he had lived to finish it.

Sources: *New Oxford American Dictionary*, *Collins COBUILD Primary Learner's Dictionary*, *Collins English Dictionary*, *The American Heritage Dictionary*

Xenophobia

This Guy

"Then <u>this</u> guy runs in, <u>drunk</u> as a bartender on his night off, screaming incomprehensible <u>blasphemies</u> and racial <u>slurs</u>. He <u>knocked</u> a hole in the wall bare-<u>fisted</u>, <u>elbowe</u>d his way to the bar, and <u>swung</u> at me with the tire iron. Complete <u>mayhem</u> broke out—first came the clowns, <u>then</u> came the elephants, then a <u>mounted policewoman</u> yelled at the crowds to move back, when suddenly and without any <u>warning</u>, the army opened fire. The blast <u>tore</u> a hole in the wall, bullets riddled the bar top, glasses <u>shattere</u>d, bottles exploded . . . It's a <u>mira-cle</u> no one was killed in the accident."

"Well, Canadians *are* notoriously <u>prickly</u> about being taken for Americans."

Sources: *New Oxford American Dictionary, Collins English Dictionary, The Home Book of Proverbs, Maxims and Familiar Phrases, Merriam-Webster's Collegiate Dictionary*

Xylophones

The Sting

"Are you OK, Ben? You're in a terrible mood—what's bugging you?"

He sighed heavily. His index finger was tracing circles on the arm of the chair.

"I'm a bit muddled, I'm not sure where to begin." He looked around to see if anyone was listening. "You must promise not to breathe a word of what I'm about to tell you."

"I am the very soul of discretion."

She leaned forward, with her elbows on the table, and he whispered in her ear. Her eyes widened with feigned shock.

"Don't think you can fool me; I wasn't born yesterday."

"Oh, I'm not joking, I promise you."

Her laughter stopped as quickly as it had begun. Her face became as hard as stone.

"Are you absolutely certain about this?"

"Would any man in his senses invent so absurd a story?"

She sat back and exhaled deeply.

"Burned to death?"

He nodded vaguely.

"Half a billion dollars?"

"That's about the size of it."

"A xylophone?"

He nodded, barely able to speak.

He took off his glasses. They sat looking at each other

196

without speaking. He leaned forward to <u>take</u> her hand, when there was a <u>crackle</u> and a whine from her microphone. He looked at her in <u>astonishment</u> as the door opened like a <u>thunderclap</u>.

Sources: *New Oxford American Dictionary, Collins COBUILD Primary Learner's Dictionary, Collins English Dictionary, The American Heritage Dictionary of Idioms*

Yy

Yearning

Orlando, FL

An astronaut's worst <u>nightmare</u> is getting detached during an extravehicle activity. Nothing for miles <u>around</u> but <u>dead</u> machinery and the <u>illimitable</u> reaches of space and time.

At the Waterside <u>Inn</u>, an <u>economy</u> motel where the pictures on the wall <u>jitter</u> whenever a truck drives by, Daniel sat staring deep into the void, reminding himself of his place in the <u>cosmos</u>. The place looked as if its caretaker had been <u>AWOL</u> for some time.

Sacrificed his family life on the <u>altar</u> of career advancement. Years of <u>arduous</u> training, one <u>ill-fated</u> expedition; then <u>boom</u>, he was fired. A swarm of ghosts <u>gyred</u> around him, a vast <u>nebular</u> cloud of <u>celestial</u> beings and <u>well-meaning</u> friends.

He climbed into his suit and sat ramrod straight in the blaze of TV lights—a feature-length documentary about the history of space flight. The man in the next room was snoring heavily.

Sources: *New Oxford American Dictionary, Collins English Dictionary, Macquarie Dictionary, The American Heritage Dictionary, Merriam-Webster's Collegiate Dictionary*

Youth

Reveille

This is it. Now or never. Speak up. Look sharp. Heave-ho. All hands on deck. The tide has turned. The jig is up. Pack your things. Say your prayers. Eat your fill. Put your best foot forward. Put the key in the ignition. Gun the engine. Raise the dust. Learn the ropes. Ascend the throne. Upset the applecart. Make friends. Make merry. Make money. Do your best. Hazard a guess. Take a chance. Take your lumps. Take to the woods. Take the ax by the handle. Raise a rebellion. Wrestle an alligator. Save a ship in distress. Keep your wits about you. Run along now. Run atilt at death. Go as fast as you can. Go, by all means. Go before I cry.

Sources: *New Oxford American Dictionary*, *Macquarie Dictionary*, *The American Heritage Dictionary*, *Merriam-Webster's Collegiate Dictionary*, *Black's Law Dictionary*

Under This Roof

Teenage angst!
Blank stares,
Cryptic messages, and
Defensive fortifications.

My eldest daughter,

Flouncing about the room, jerking her
shoulders, gesticulating.

It's no good trying.

On the one hand, we can appeal for peace, and on the other,
declare war.

Difficult if not impossible,

The journey from youth to maturity.

Poor kid.

Landlocked sailor.

The doors are made against you.

But I've got news for you—

And I have it on good authority—

The hours pass quickly,

The pawn queens,

The answer rests with you.

The strong, silent type,

Five feet tall,

With unblinking frankness.

My attempts are in vain:

A carefully worded reply, and

An X-rated gesture.

Your typical teenager,

At the zenith of her powers.

Source: *Merriam-Webster's Collegiate Dictionary*

Yuletide

My True Love Gave to Me

Twelve <u>labours</u> of Hercules,
Eleven gallons of <u>diesel</u>,
Ten <u>head</u> of cattle,
Nine breeding <u>pairs</u> of birds,
Eight <u>M</u>bytes of memory,
<u>Seventh-Day</u> Baptists,
Six months of <u>unclouded</u> happiness,
Five <u>venturous</u> young men,

Four slices of bread,

Three spoons of sugar,

Two fundamentally different concepts of democracy,

And a sin in the eyes of God.

Sources: *New Oxford American Dictionary, Macquarie Dictionary, Collins COBUILD Primary Learner's Dictionary*

Zz

Zen

Guided Meditation

Take a deep <u>breath</u>, sit <u>back</u>, and relax. Be <u>quiet</u>. <u>Free</u> your mind and body of excess tension. Is something <u>bother</u>ing you? You don't <u>have</u> to explain. Keeping your mouth closed, breathe in through your <u>nostril</u>s. <u>Let</u> go of stress. <u>Shut</u> up.

Don't allow impatience to <u>tempt</u> you. There's a <u>time</u> for everything—be <u>lost</u> to all sense of duty, <u>abstract</u> the notions of time, of space, and of matter, <u>relinquish</u> your hold on the processes of the <u>mind</u>. See things as they <u>really</u> are. <u>Breathe</u> in slowly. <u>Let</u> out a scream.

Imagine for a moment that you're living in an <u>ideal</u> world. A world overrun by <u>zombies</u>—<u>pardon</u> me—a world of mystery and <u>enchantment</u>. Try to breathe <u>normally</u>. There are no tears, no <u>recrimination</u>s. You are immersed in an illusory, yet <u>sensate</u>, world. <u>Inward</u> peace, <u>freedom</u> from fear—

I'm sorry, I've <u>broken</u> a glass. I just <u>zoned</u> out for a moment, I'm ever so sorry.

<u>Breathe</u> in through your nose. Please <u>step</u> this way. I'll take you to the <u>secret</u> spring. I don't mind <u>how</u> long you take. Feel free to wander around as you <u>please</u>. You can relax on the veranda as the sun <u>sinks</u>. Sit down and make yourself at <u>home</u>. Dinner is <u>ready</u>.

Sources: *New Oxford American Dictionary, Macquarie Dictionary, Collins COBUILD Primary Learner's Dictionary*

Zombies

Miranda

"What do you want to do for the rest of your life?"

She looked at him in astonishment.

"I don't want to be stuck in an office all my life! I'd like to be somebody!"

He laughed heartily and pushed the button for the twentieth floor. The elevator dropped like a stone.

She felt belittled. She felt unwanted. Miranda felt a wistful longing for the old days, when people believed to have the power to zombify a person were widely feared and respected.

Source: *New Oxford American Dictionary*

TELL THE WORLD THIS BOOK WAS		
GOOD	BAD	SO-SO
		206

Acknowledgments

This book would still be an idea I wistfully forced on strangers at parties, were it not for a formidable crew of smart and huge-hearted people to whom I'll be forever grateful.

My agent, Ted Weinstein, patiently helped turn a pile of directionless notes into a proposal and found a home for it at Harper Perennial. My editor, Hannah Robinson, made invaluable contributions and answered a thousand questions with grace and good humour as that proposal became a manuscript. Thanks to them both, and to everybody at Harper—particularly Leydiana Rodriguez, who has the patience of a saint. Thanks also to copyeditor Julie Hersh, who is quite possibly superhuman.

Austin Kleon introduced me to Ted and gave advice generously. Erin McKean sat down with me to talk dictionaries and pointed me in a thousand fascinating directions. Robin Sloan, together with Austin and Erin, wrote extraordinarily kind things about the book in its infancy. I am enormously grateful to all three of them.

Having skulked around on its periphery for a few months, I was warmly welcomed into the lexicography community by Jane Solomon, Kory Stamper, Katherine Connor Martin, and Ben Zimmer. Thanks to them for their time, expertise, support, and for teaching me the secret handshake.

Thanks to Kenny Meyers for technical expertise and friendship; Daniel Levin Becker for a burrito lunch and a book's worth of inspiration; Tom Rosenthal and Phil Smith for musical accompaniment; Daniel Agee, Matt Buchanan, and Dan Cassaro for making me look good; and the staff of San Francisco's Mechanic's Institute Library for their assistance.

Thanks to Anna Hurley, for love and patience.

Thanks to my family, friends, and anybody who supported the project, or had the misfortune to spend time with me in the months when the book was being written—there are entirely too many of you to list, but I'll make sure you know who you are the next time I see you, and every time thereafter.

Finally, thanks to the intrepid lexicographers responsible for the dictionaries referenced in this book—it truly would not exist without your diligent drudgery.

About the Author

Jez Burrows is a British designer, illustrator, and writer. He studied graphic design at the University of Brighton and has since created work for the *New York Times*, Facebook, WNYC, *Monocle*, *WIRED*, Cards Against Humanity, and others. He lives in San Francisco and enjoys long moonlit walks through the dictionary.